Great Unsolved
Mystery Of
1826

By David W. Firmes

THE GREAT UNSOLVED MYSTERY OF 1826

This is a work of fiction. Many locations are real and some of the historical events depicted actually took place but some of the events in those locations are from the imagination of the author. Some of the individuals referred to are real but any dialogue relating to those individuals is the fabrication of the author to create this work of fiction.

"NOBODY HAS ANY CONSCIENCE ABOUT
ADDING TO THE IMPROBABILITIES OF A
MARVELOUS TALE."

NATHANIEL HAWTHORNE

***

Dedicated to my wife Suzanne who has been very patient through the years while I have satisfied my writing aspirations!

INTRODUCTION

Summer 1965 - Mount Washington Valley

To update the reader: Seven years have passed since the renowned bibliophile, turned private investigator Gallagher Brady, burst onto the scene in the quaint little town of Jackson, New Hampshire, which lies nestled in the shadows of Agiocochook, a.k.a. Mount Washington. Gallagher's presence in the valley had become widely known when he began investigating the strange case of the 'Thorn Hill Covenant' with his companion Jonathan Henry. The investigation opened up a Pandora's Box for Gallagher personally and the ripple effect became nationwide. Before the ink could dry from Jonathan's pen while relating that mysterious case on paper, dead fish were being found in the Saco and Swift rivers causing wildlife to die from their consumption of dead fish. The two returned to their investigating talents once again, which led to a series of events, which has come to be known as the Tale of Two Rivers.

By the end of 1962, both Gallagher and Jonathan were able to return to their respective occupations, which has been a welcome relief to them and their families. Gallagher has been able to continue his hunt for rare and hard to find works of literature to add to the Blackthorn Antiquarian Museum located in the center of Jackson. He has also been able to find time to oversee his bookshop, The Turning Page with his wife Anna. They have regularly invited the youth of the valley to visit the bookshop on Saturday mornings to listen to the reading of selected stories, which has caused many of the children in the valley to become avid readers themselves to the delight of their parents.

Jonathan has continued writing down his exploits with Gallagher while at the same time contributing selected newsworthy events for the Jackson Observer as a freelance journalist.

Gallagher's Aunt Helen, without telling anyone, secretly married Bill Waters who was a family friend, which was a surprise to Gallagher and all who know her. She at one time said she had resigned herself to being without a husband until her final breath because there wasn't a man she ever met that appealed to her. Bill, not a particularly handsome man but very kind and considerate, was able to bring out the caring and loving side of her as she later admitted. Bill sold his house in Lincoln and the newlyweds moved into the carriage house at Eagle House by the insistence of Gallagher and Anna. Helen was delighted to be able to stay on in her childhood home.

Calmness returned to the valley and the summer of '65' proved to be one to remember for the tranquility and restfulness the residents of the valley have been able to enjoy. It was not until the fall of that year that an interesting discovery took place in Crawford Notch. This is the subject of our story and it begins this way.

***

PART 1

THE DISCOVERY

1

Autumn - 1965

Gallagher woke from a restful night's sleep on a tranquil Sunday morning with great anticipation of hiking the Mount Willey Trail, which is one of many four thousand foot hikes that grace the White Mountains. Gallagher, realizing Anna had already been up for a while, walked downstairs into the kitchen where she was found cooking up a big breakfast of blueberry pancakes and sweet maple cured bacon. From behind, he lovingly put his arms around her and said, "Good morning. I see you're preparing us well for our hike. Remember we also need to pack enough food to cover the duration of our hike for the next two to three days."

Anna laughed and said, "You haven't even had your breakfast yet and you are already thinking about food for the hike."

"There's nothing wrong in being prepared. Think of the Boy Scout's motto.

"And what was that I might ask, being I was girl scout and we had our motto."

"Be prepared!"

"Funny, we had the same motto. I'm sure the boy and girl scouts would be proud of us because we are all packed and ready to go."

"We are definitely a team."

"Are we going to combine Mount Willey with Field, Avalon and Tom?"

"Absolutely! The four mountains make a perfect hike for this time of year. We better pack some rain gear too because they are predicting some showers later this afternoon."

Anna walked over to the big picture window overlooking the valley and said, "It's hard to believe they're talking rain on such a beautiful looking morning. There's not a cloud in the sky."

Gallagher nods his head. "You know how these mountains can whip up winds very quickly and carry any moisture along with it. It's better to be safe than sorry."

"You're right as usual..."

***

AMC's Ethan Pond Campsite is located at the base of Mount Willey, along the Ethan Pond Trail. Gallagher parked his Land Rover in the lot specified for overnight hikers. Gallagher and Anna hiked most of the day enjoying cloudless skies then around dusk decided to set up camp because clouds started drifting in from the west. Gallagher looked up at the sky and said, "It looks like rain is coming in those dark clouds. We better move our camp off trail and go deeper into the woods to get as much shelter as we can; this spot has quite a history.

Anna studied the trail map and said, "You're right. According to where we are on this map; we are right on top of where the Willey landslide took place."

"That is not a very comforting thought," Gallagher replies while looking down the mountain. "I can see the scaring along the rock face from that infamous slide. Hopefully the rains will go easy on Willey tonight."

They made their way deeper into the woods and then the rains started falling fast and hard. "Let's get the tent up right away," Gallagher declared.

For the next three hours, the rain came down in torrents. Gallagher and Anna kept dry inside the tent while waiting for the storm to pass. Off in the distance they heard the roar of thunder and saw lightning light up the darkened sky from inside their tent. Gallagher waited several minutes then he peered out of the tent to see if the sky was clearing. "It looks like the storm is heading northeast. I can see a sliver of the moon in the western sky. I think we can rest here for the night and start up again in the morning."

"Sounds good...I packed some bread, cheese and a bottle of Cabernet. All we need now is a fire." Gallagher shrugged his shoulders and said, "If we had some dry wood, it would work quite well. We will just have to eat by candlelight and imagine it's the warm glow of a fire."

Gallagher poured each of them a glass of wine and started thinking to himself about what happened back in 1826 on the same spot where they had just pitched their tent for the night. He looks over at Anna and says, "I'm sure you know the story of the Willey tragedy."

"I remember learning about it in school but the details I had chosen to forget. It was a horrible tragedy and one I hope never happens again in this peaceful valley. I know the Willey House can be visited on Route 302 but I have never gone there to see it."

"It's amazing how many sights and attractions can be in our own backyard and we just take them for granted because we know they will always be there whenever we decide to visit them."

"I think you're the exception when it comes to appreciating what's around you."

"I think it all stems from when I almost missed out on all that's here when I was taken away to

England at such an early age. The English countryside was wonderful but to me these mountains really call to me. I feel secure for some reason next to them."

"It sounds like a contradiction when you think about it. The Willey family was not too secure."

Gallagher takes a sip of wine. "If you don't mind let me tell you the story as I had heard it told by my grandfather. He had been told a firsthand account by someone who was there after the tragedy."

"I don't know if I want to hear it."

"We are safe here," Gallagher assures. "The rain has slowed down so Willey will be calm tonight."

"Okay. You have a captive audience."

Gallagher begins: *"During the fall of 1825, Samuel Willey, Jr. of Bartlett moved into a small house in the heart of Crawford Notch with his wife, five children, and two hired men. The first year, the three men enlarged and improved the house, which the family operated as an Inn to accommodate travelers through the mountains on the desolate notch road. A little cluster of buildings were situated in the shadow of what is now called Mount Willey.*

In June, following a heavy rain, the Willeys were terrified when they witnessed a great mass of soil and vegetation, torn loose from the mountainside across the river, slide in a path of destruction to the valley floor. As a result, Mr. Willey built a cave-like shelter a short distance above the house to which the family could flee if a slide threatened their side of the valley. During the night of August 28, 1826, after a long drought, which had dried the mountain soil to an unusual depth, came one of the most violent and destructive rainstorms ever recorded in the White Mountains. The Saco River had risen twenty feet overnight sweeping livestock away, farms set afloat, and great gorges were cut in the mountains. Two days after the storm, anxious friends and relatives penetrated the debris-strewn valley to learn the fate of the Willey family. They found the house unharmed, but the surrounding fields covered with debris. Huge boulders, trees, and masses of soil been swept from Mt. Willey's newly bared slopes. The house escaped damage because of being just below a ledge that divided the major slide into two streams. The split caused the slide to pass by the house on both sides leaving it untouched. Inside, beds appeared hurriedly left and a Bible lay on the table.

Mr. and Mrs. Willey, two of the children, and both hired men were found nearby, crushed in the wreckage of the slide. They found the bodies buried near the house and later moved them to Conway. Three children and the family dog were never found. If the family had stayed in their home, they would have lived."

Anna completely mesmerized by the story finally said after Gallagher finished, "You tell that story like you were the one that was there."

"My grandfather must have told me that story at least a half dozen times. Helen reminded me of it when we lived in England after a horrible storm hit the mountain area where we lived. It seems to have been burnt into my memory."

They both finished their wine and cuddled up and eventually fell asleep under a blanket of stars and the sound of tree frogs and crickets.

***

The following morning Gallagher woke up first and wandered outside the tent and quickly noticed a large depression in the side of the mountain below them. Anna heard a gasp and realized it was Gallagher, who was standing right outside the tent.

"Gallagher...is anything the matter?"

"It looks like the heavy rains of last night created a giant sinkhole in the side of the mountain."

Anna joins Gallagher and says, "Why don't I cook us some breakfast and then we can take a closer look."

"Sounds good..."

***

After a breakfast of sausage and eggs, they made their way down to the entrance of the large opening in the mountain. "This is very strange," Gallagher declared. "It looks like a cave, which is not on any trail map I've ever seen."

"How about the cave you mentioned last night that Mr. Willey built as a place to hide in case there was a landslide? Could this be it? The landslide could have covered the cave over and now the storm last night washed all the rocks away."

"It might have because I don't remember ever seeing it before. I hiked this same trail last year with your brother Scott and it was not here. The heavy rains of last night must have loosened the rocks away from the entrance to the cave."

"Do you think we should go inside and take a look?" Anna asked hesitantly.

"Okay, but we need to watch our footing. We don't want another slide to bury us inside."

They slowly made their way inside the cave and Gallagher noticed the walls of the cave were solid rock, almost as if it was made by human hands.

"I think you're right," Gallagher admits. "This may be what Mr. Willey built. I thought it was just a shelter under a ledge; not a cave."

Gallagher entered the cave and declared, "This is really strange." He walked further in while shining his flashlight along the wall to guide them then he suddenly stopped in his tracks when his light fell upon the skeletal remains of a human body.

"What do you see?" Anna asked.

"A body...!" Gallagher draws closer and notices the person is amazingly preserved inside the clothing

13

of what he or she was wearing. "By the type of dress it appears to be a man's body."

Gallagher kneels down and notices the man is clutching onto a leather pouch next to his chest. Gallagher slowly releases it from the boney hand and carefully opens it up.

"What's inside?" Anna asks as she comes slowly closer. Gallagher reaches into the pouch and pulls an object out. "You're not going to believe this but it appears to be a gold wedding ring. This man may have been on his way to propose to his fiancé because it's a women's ring."

Gallagher examines the ring carefully. "There are some words written on the inside of the band."

"What does it say?"

Gallagher held his flashlight up to the ring and read it aloud. "Dieu et mon Droit."

"Is there any name?"

"Only the four words..."

"Do you know what the words mean?"

"The words are written in French and mean, 'God and My Right'. We better cut our hike short and get back to Jackson right away. Doctor Mathews needs to examine these remains right away. He will have his work cut out for him because this body may have been here as far back as 1826 when the landslide took place."

They packed up their gear and headed back to Eagle House. As soon as Gallagher walked into the house, he immediately went to the phone and called Jonathan.

***

2

"Jonathan, its Gallagher. Can you come over right away? Anna and I just found the remains of a man's body inside a cave up on Mount Willey. He apparently has been buried there for years; by all appearances. The body has been left untouched for a forensic team to examine it but what is even more interesting is the dead man was holding onto a leather pouch containing a women's gold wedding ring. I have it here for you to see."

"I'll be right over."

***

While Gallagher was waiting for Jonathan to arrive, he went into his library and pulled out a book of short stories by Nathaniel Hawthorne. Anna walked in and asked, "What are you looking up?"

"I remember reading the story of the 'Ambitious Guest' by Nathaniel Hawthorne when I was a boy. The story is a work of fiction but is based on the Willey landslide. By grandfather urged me to read it right after he related the Willey tragedy to me."

"What are you looking for in particular?"

"Not quite sure. I know the identity of the guest referred to in the story is never mentioned by name."

"But you said it was a work of fiction so what difference does it make?"

"Yes I did, but I wonder if it was really fiction."

Gallagher begins reading a brief synopsis of the story written on the inside cover of the book to Anna. "Listen to this."

'A young traveler stops for the night with a family that lives in a "notch" next to a mountain. They make friendly conversation, interrupted once by the sound of a wagon carrying other travelers who pause but do not go inside, continuing on with their journey and then by the sound of rocks falling from the slope. The father reassures the visitor that rockslides happen regularly without causing harm, but that the family has a "safe place" to go in the event of a serious collapse.

The group carries on with their friendly conversation. The visitor acknowledges that he is young and has no accomplishments of note, but hopes he will have "achieved my destiny" before he dies and then "I shall have built my monument!" The father expresses the wish for a more humble legacy, and the aged grandmother makes a request for her dying day. The outdoor weather corresponds to his mixed emotions.

Suddenly they hear the sound of a much larger avalanche. They scream in fear of "The Slide!" and bolt outside for their safe place. However, they all are caught up in the rockslide and killed, while the house is completely undamaged. Their bodies swept away and never found. The narrator notes that some who see the house later think there is evidence of a visitor that night, but others disagree - the young man has in fact died without leaving any trace of his life.'

~

Anna is speechless after hearing Hawthorne's tale then after giving some thought finally speaks up and says, "Are you thinking what I'm thinking?"

Gallagher reveals a slight smile and says, "I know it sounds crazy but the ambitious guest in Hawthorne's story may be the man in the cave."

"Could he be? Is that really possible?"

"I think Jonathan may be able to shed some light on this with his resources at the Jackson Observer. They must have records going back that far listing any missing persons in this area."

"When was the Observer founded?"

"Let me see, I have today's edition right here on my desk." Gallagher looks at the front page. "The paper was founded in 1801."

"What if Jonathan comes up empty? Is there anywhere else we can look?"

Gallagher thinks for a moment. "There are only three, maybe four people I know of still living in the

17

valley who may have heard or talked to someone who lived at the time of the Willey tragedy."

"Who are they?"

"The landslide happened in 1826. My great-grandfather, Graham Blackthorn was living then. Helen told me Graham had even helped in recovering some of the bodies."

"That's what you meant by a firsthand account. Your great grandfather Graham told your grandfather Jonas about what he saw."

"That's right. Graham obviously told Jonas about the landslide; and what he did to help in the recovery. Jonas personally knew Bill Waters, Professor Meridian, Chief John Peterson and Daisy Saffron and he may have related the experience to them in conversation. It is a long shot but maybe one of them remembers something Jonas might have said about the landslide that can help us. Can you wait for Jonathan? I think Valerie is coming over with him to see you. Show Jonathan the ring. I will head over to the Professor's house and start picking his brain.

"Okay. While you're there, let me know how the Professor's new home is coming along; I heard it was almost finished."

"I heard it's done. As soon as Louise and Dr. Dredmeyer were married he needed his space again for his research so he didn't delay the rebuilding of his home after the fire. He also added on an addition."

"Who would have thought the doctor would ever get married. He had been a confirmed bachelor all his life. He said he was too busy in his research to have a wife."

Gallagher replies with a big smile, "All he needed was to see a woman's touch around the home when Louise and the Professor lived with him while the their house was being rebuilt; it was just a matter of time."

"I'm so happy for them both. Louise has always been tied to her father and his needs and she never had the time for romance. I'm just wondering how the Professor will cope with being alone."

"Rumor has it, his daughter in Sugar Hill is moving in with him so she can keep an eye on him. That's why he added on an addition. It will also be good for the Professor to be around his grandson. He used to grumble about hardly ever seeing him."

"Who told you that little bit of gossip?"

Gallagher smiles and says, "Who else but Lars and Gus at the Tavern."

'I might have guessed. Who has to go to the beauty parlor anymore to find out the latest gossip in town?"

***

Gallagher starts walking towards the front door of the Professor's newly rebuilt home and noticed him working in the backyard. "Professor, how are you doing on this beautiful summer day? The sky is crystal clear after the rains the other night and it's a perfect day for tending a garden."

"Gallagher, it's so good to see you. It is a gorgeous day for sure. Can I offer you some of my last remaining tomatoes of the season before the first frost finishes them off?"

"I would love some. Do you have a few minutes? I need to ask you a few questions."

"Sure, I need a break anyways; my back is killing me. I am not as young as my mind thinks I am. Let us sit over there on the patio. I have a pitcher of freshly made lemonade."

They both sat under a large oak tree, which is in the centerpiece of the patio. "What can I help you with my good friend?"

Gallagher hands a book of short stories to the Professor and says, "Do you know the story of the Ambitious Guest?"

"By Nathaniel Hawthorne; I've read it a number of times. You know it's based on the famous Willey landslide?"

"Yes I know. My grandfather had me read it after telling me about the tragedy. And I also remember Helen telling me about my great grandfather, Graham Blackthorn and his involvement in recovering some of the bodies."

"Really...! Jonas never spoke of it to me."

"I was afraid you were going to say that but anyways; Anna and I found a dead body inside a cave up on Mount Willey. We were caught in the heavy rainstorm of the other night and after it was over we started out again in the morning and we came across the cave, which had been uncovered by the heavy streams of water coming down from the mountain. We entered the cave and found the remains of a man's body that was holding onto a leather pouch that contained a women's gold wedding ring."

The Professor's interest suddenly peaked and exclaimed, "Dead man and a women's wedding ring...! Do you have it with you?"

Gallagher surprised at the Professor's reaction says, "Sorry...I don't. Jonathan is coming by the house to check it out."

"Is there anything else you can tell me about the ring?"

"Inside the gold band were four words etched into the soft gold, 'Dieu et mon Droit'"

The Professor looked up at Gallagher astounded by his words. "Do you know old French?"

"I know some French. Remember I did attend Oxford."

"Very good; the motto is old French for literally "God and my right"."

"I knew that much" Gallagher replies.

"It means the king is "Rex Angliae Die Gratia" King of England by the Grace of God."

"If it has to do with England why is it written in French?"

"For the Royal Coat of Arms of the Kingdom of England to have a French motto was not unusual, given that Norman French was the primary language of the English Royal Court."

"Are you telling me the ring may have had something to do with the King of England?"

"Sounds a little crazy but if the man you found in the cave goes back to the time of the Willey landslide, anything is possible. Do you know the legend of Nancy?"

Gallagher thinks for a moment. "I can't say I have heard of that one. How does the legend go?"

"I know you're familiar with the Crawford Notch area and it was at the point where a stream came down from a mountain into a large ravine where a girl by the name of Nancy was found frozen to death in a shroud of snow in the fall of 1788. She had set out alone from Jefferson in search of a young farmer who was to have married her, and walked thirty miles through trackless snow between sunset and dawn. Then her strength gave out and she sank beside the road never to rise again. Her devoted young beau went mad with remorse when he learned of the manner of her death and he did not long survive her. It has been told in folklore that men who have traversed the savage passes of the Notch on chilly nights in October have fancied that they heard, above the clash of the stream and whispering of the woods, long, shuddering groans mingled with despairing cries and gibbering laughter."

"Wow...what a story! Did you have some thought as to whether the ring might be connected to that love affair?"

"Well the thought did cross my mind at first but it could not be for one reason; the farmer died and was found somewhere else."

"So who could this ring belong to and who was the intended receiver?"

"I think you better get Jonathan on this one. He can probably find something in the Observer's archives. Maybe there's a listing of upcoming engagements in that year. Maybe even a missing persons report."

Gallagher looks at his watch and says, "I've already thought of that and Jonathan should be arriving at Eagle House any moment now. Thanks for the lemonade and the tomatoes. I need to get back right away before he leaves."

"Let me know what you find out. This sounds real mysterious." Gallagher nods and says, "What else is new? Mysterious events seem to find me."

The Professor laughs and says, "Remember, you found this mystery, it did not find you." Gallagher laughs and says, "Thanks for making that clear."

***

3

Gallagher arrived back at Eagle House and found Jonathan having ice tea with Helen, Bill and Anna.

"Can I join the tea party?" Gallagher said as he walked into the kitchen. Anna quickly speaks up and asks, "What did you find out?"

"Nothing that will help identify the man we found in the cave but I did hear an interesting story about Nancy."

Jonathan looks at Gallagher and asks, "Nancy who?"

"Never mind; it's not important. Did you get filled in on what we need from you?"

"Yes. I am going to search the archives at the newspaper and I will let Chief Perry know about the body in the cave. Doctor Mathews and his forensic team might be able to shed some light on who the victim was so many years ago."

Gallagher nods and says, "I know back in the early fifties Watson and Crick were the scientists to figure out the structure of DNA, the written code unique to each individual living organism. It was recognized that someday in the future the usefulness of DNA testing would be used for forensic investigations but regretfully that time as not yet arrived."

"Maybe a jeweler will be able to help us find out where the ring may have come from or at least how old it is," Jonathan declared.

 Gallagher nods again then looks at Helen. "Do you remember telling me about your grandfather, Graham Blackthorn, helping in the retrieval of the bodies after the Willey landslide?"

"Yes I do. What about it?"

"Well, in Nathaniel Hawthorne's story of the 'Ambitious Guest' he relates about an unknown visitor who also died in the landslide. I can't get it out of my head that it may be possible he knew of someone visiting the Inn on that night but never spoke of him by name?"

"Are you thinking the man you found in the cave could be the same man?"

"I know it's a long shot knowing Hawthorne's story is fiction based on something factual such as the Willey tragedy but it's something to think about."

Jonathan's wheels start turning and says, "I wonder if we could find out more about Hawthorne himself?"

"What are you getting at?" Gallagher asked with mounting interest.

"If we find out more about his life maybe we can find a clue somewhere, which may point to the identity of the guest in his story."

Helen starts laughing and says, "I believe you two have got this investigative bug of yours out of control. The story is fiction, plain and simple. I am surprised you are not thinking about investigating who the man was who killed the man with the ugly eye in Poe's story of the Tell Tale Heart. You know the one who was murdered and buried in the floor."

Gallagher shakes his head and says, "There's no mystery there. The murderer tore up the floorboards in Poe's story. There's nothing to investigate; he admitted the deed."

"So you're really going to pursue this?" Helen asked revealing her amusement at the notion.

Gallagher smiles..."This mystery is more to my liking. It is not dealing with the FBI or the CIA or Fifth Column or the Russians. It's a genuine, whatever happened, who done it mystery."

***

4

Gallagher's next person to talk to on his list is Daisy Saffron. After her son Mario returned home to stay, she decided to keep the Trading Post open and enjoy the remaining years of her life in Harts Location, where all her ancestors were buried.

Gallagher enters the Trading Post and sees Daisy tucked in a corner reading a mystery novel. "Is it a Dasheill Hammett or Mickey Spillane?"

Daisy looks up from her book and says, "Neither one; it's a Dick Francis novel titled 'Nerve'. I can hardly put the book down."

"Daisy, you say that about every mystery story you read. How is Mario doing these days? I heard he's been helping Little Hands on his farm."

"Gallagher, it's so good to see you; it's been awhile. Mario is doing just great. I only need him on weekends to help here. He likes working the farm with Little Hands and so between books I'm knitting him a sweater so when the cold winds of winter come breezing through the Notch he'll be nice and warm."

"Nothing compares to a mother's love," Gallagher declared. "The reason why I've come by is not only

26

to see you but to ask you a couple questions regarding the Willey landslide."

"The Willey landslide...? I am afraid that's even before my time. I may look old but hopefully not that old."

Gallagher laughs and says, "You know I didn't mean that but you knew my grandfather Jonas and I was wondering if he had ever talked with you about the tragedy and how his father, Graham Blackthorn, helped in the retrieval of the bodies."

Daisy pauses for a moment. "I don't ever remember him talking to me about it but there's something I do remember hearing about, which I don't believe it was ever solved."

"What was never solved?"

"Shortly after the tragedy two families who lived here in Harts Location packed up and left the area almost overnight and have not been heard of since. I remember hearing it from my father who knew the families well."

"Did he ever tell you their names or where exactly they lived in Harts Location?"

"If he did, I don't remember. Even if he did, you know how stories can change the more they have spread to others. I was very young and I did not really care much about it at the time, like most kids my age. I am sorry Gallagher, my memory is drying up. Remember I am getting close to ninety. I'm happy if I remember where I left my false teeth."

"I never knew you wore false teeth."

Daisy laughs. "See what I mean. I never wear them because usually I can't find them."

Gallagher laughs and says, "Well the little you've told me is a beginning."

"Have you tried talking with John Peterson? He might have heard about the missing families."

"Not yet but he's next on my list. He knew my grandfather well and maybe he will remember something."

"It's worth a try. I will ask around and if I hear or think of anything more, I'll call you."

"Thanks Daisy. Give my best to Mario."

***

Gallagher left the trading post with another question to think about. Without leaving any word, who were the families who left the area right after the landslide and were never heard from again?

Gallagher was a little apprehensive about going to John Peterson's home because he knew very well his wife fears for him whenever he gets involved in any police work at his age and his frail health. Gallagher knocks on the door and John opens it to Gallagher's surprise and relief. "Hi Chief... Is your wife around?"

Peterson cannot help but laugh and says, "Gallagher...are you having an affair with my wife? I know how you love her cookies."

Gallagher returns a laugh and says, "Yes...I mean...I do love her cookies but seriously I was hoping she wasn't around. I have to ask you a few questions about the Willey landslide and I know how upset she gets lately when you get involved in police work."

"Come into my study. Margaret is visiting her sister in Lincoln. I do not expect her back until tomorrow. Can I get you something?"

"No thanks Chief."

"Please Gallagher, call me John. Tom Perry is the Chief now. I'm retired for good this time."

"I know...John; it's a hard habit to break. You had been Chief as far back as my grandfather's time, which is what brings me here today. Do you remember any details regarding the Willey landslide other than the immediate family and two hired hands being killed?"

"We had some police records dating back that far but age had destroyed much of the print. They were not very legible to begin with."

"Does anything stand out in your mind?"

"Nothing from those records but there was something your grandfather mentioned to me one time. He said his father was very distraught over a story he read in a magazine called 'The New England' back in...let me think...I believe it was around 1847 or 48."

Gallagher's raises his brow after hearing those words. "Was it the Ambitious Guest?"

"That's it; it was written by that famous author who wrote The Scarlet Letter. What was his name?"

"Nathaniel Hawthorne."

"That's right. I remember him telling me your great grandfather felt the story was disrespectful of the dead."

"It was only fiction; granted the story was based on the Willey tragedy but it was not disrespectful to the family. It was more of paying homage to the family. Why would he get so upset?"

"It had nothing to do with the family but with the guest. It's all I can remember, I'm sorry."

"With the guest...? The story was only fiction. Well anyways, that's still a help. I'm sorry to have bothered you."

"No bother at all. It is good to see you. It has been awhile. What are you investigating these days?"

"To make a long story short, Anna and I found a body in a cave on Mount Willey when we were hiking recently. I'm trying to find out if the body could be the so called 'ambitious guest' in Hawthorne's story."

"Wow, wouldn't that be something but don't you think that's a bit of a stretch?"

"It may be but it's worth looking into."

"Well I wish you success in your hunt for answers. If I think of anything else I will give you a call."

"Thanks Chief...I mean John."

***

Gallagher left Peterson's home with his head spinning from what he had just heard. Was there

30

really a guest and could it be the man in the cave? What did Hawthorne know? Why was his great-grandfather so upset? Those were the questions Gallagher needed answered. Gallagher was hoping Jonathan was able to come up with something to help solve the mystery.

* * *

5

Gallagher returned to Eagle House filled with more questions than answers. He sees Helen and Bill sitting in the living room and joins them looking exhausted.

"It looks like you've been climbing another mountain today," Helen declared after noticing the look of weariness on Gallagher's face.

"You don't know the half of it."

"What have you found out?"

"I talked to the Professor Meridian, Daisy Saffron and John Peterson and have come up with two more unanswered questions. Who are the two families who disappeared from the valley right after the Willey tragedy? Also, Grandpa Graham was upset over Hawthorne's story of the Ambitious Guest, which seems a bit odd because it was only a work of fiction." Gallagher pauses... "Or was it?"

Helen suddenly gets up from the couch and leaves the room as if it were on fire. Bill looks at Gallagher and says, "Ever since you started investigating this thing Helen's mind has been preoccupied with

31

trying to remember what she knew or heard about the tragedy."

At that moment, Jonathan enters the room with a big grin on his face and says, "I think I may have found something. We need to travel to Lake Sebago."

"Lake Sebago in Maine...?" Gallagher asked surprised.

"The town of Raymond to be exact...."

"What did you find?"

"Hawthorne lived in Raymond just before he moved back to the town of his birth, which was Salem, Massachusetts."

Helen overhearing Jonathan as she returns to the room holding a book in her hand says, "If you take Rte. 302 from Harts Location and drive southeast you will drive right through the town of Raymond. It's approximately 66 miles from the site of the Willey landslide."

Bill Waters looked at Helen with awe and asked, "How can you possibly know that off the top of your head?"

"That *would* be amazing but what I did remember was this journal which belonged to my grandfather, Graham Blackthorn. I happened to stumbled across it in the attic right before I left for England with Gallagher back in 1944. It made little sense to me then but with the recent experience Gallagher and Anna just had up on Mount Willey; it jogged my memory about what I read in this journal so long ago."

Helen hands the journal to Gallagher. "I placed a marker where I believe you will find his notations to be very interesting."

Gallagher turns to the page and begins reading the passage Helen had marked:

Date: August 28, 1826

On my second trip to Raymond, I stopped in to see a former schoolmate of mine who had graduated with me from Bowdoin College. When I left Eagle House at 4:00 in the morning the sky was darkening in the western sky and the air had a heavy wetness feeling on my face. The purpose of my visit was to offer my advice to him over an argument he recently had with his fiancé. The weather was just a minor inconvenience and it did not hold me back from traveling to his home. When I arrived four hours later my friend had just had a visit with a mutual friend of ours named Nathaniel, who used to live down the street. His visit was regarding the same problem our friend was having with his fiancé and he advised him to travel and see her immediately with a proposal of marriage; that very day if possible. He showed me the wedding ring he intended to give her, a solid gold wedding band. I agreed with our friend Nathaniel that he should travel to the Notch before it was too late, and said no more about it the rest of my visit. We reminisced about our school days over tea and sandwiches. I left after a couple hours and headed back to Eagle House confident he was going to offer his hand in marriage to the love of his life that very night. His horse and carriage was being prepared for the four-hour journey just as I was leaving.

On my journey home, my horse pulled up lame so I had to spend the night at an Inn on the shores of Moose Pond. The weather was threatening in the western sky and I was happy to be off the road for the night but I knew in my heart my dear friend would travel through it all to meet with the only love of his life and ask for her hand in marriage....

Tears had formed on Gallagher's face when he put the journal down. "Helen...how come you didn't remember reading this before?"

"Like I said, with all that was going on at the time I had to get you out of Eagle House right away before those Nazi's on the train showed up. I simply put it out of my mind. Since you mentioned what you found in the cave I've been racking my brain trying to remember where I heard of all this before."

Gallagher picked up the journal and handed it to Jonathan. "Did you notice the date?"

Jonathan nods in disbelief and says almost choking on his words, "The same exact date of the landslide."

***

6

The next day Gallagher arrived at the police station and saw Chief Perry sitting at his desk talking on the phone. Perry gestures Gallagher to sit and indicates with his watch he would be just a minute.

Perry finally hung up the phone, looked at Gallagher, and said, "That was Doctor Matthews and he just finished with his examination of the body you found in the cave and he said the man, according to the condition of his teeth, was approximately twenty to twenty-five years of age when he died of suffocation."

Gallagher takes a piece of paper out of his pocket and writes down what Perry just told him. "That's very interesting. Hawthorne started attending Bowdoin College in 1821 and graduated in 1825 then moved back to Salem, Massachusetts.

Perry, not knowing what Gallagher was getting at asks, "You mean Hawthorne the author."

"That's right."

"What does he have to do with the man in the cave?"

"That's what I'm trying to find out. My great-grandfather kept a journal of his travels and in it we found a notation written down describing a visit he had with a former schoolmate of his who planned to travel up to Crawford Notch on that very night to propose to his fiancé. It even mentioned a gold wedding ring he was bringing with him to propose to her. According to the journal my great grandfather graduated with the unknown man and Hawthorne."

"He didn't mention his name?"

"No, just referred to him as a former schoolmate."

"On what night did he travel to the Notch?"

"August 28th, 1826."

"You're kidding. When was your great grandfather born?"

"According to our family records he was born the same year as Hawthorne in 1804."

"How old was he when he married your great-grandmother."

Gallagher starts laughing. "He was apparently a regular Don Juan. He married her when he was seventy-six years old. She was only twenty-five. My grandfather Jonas was born in 1880. Jonas was thirty-two in 1912 when he drafted the infamous Thorn Hill Covenant."

"You know you should write a book."

"No, not me; I just like reading them."

"So what's your next move?"

"Good question. I think a trip to Salem might be in order."

***

Gallagher arrived back at Eagle House and immediately walked into his library and pulled out the collection of short stories by Hawthorne called 'Twice-Told Tales'. He opened it to the inside cover and read the year of its first publication; 1837. He then went back outside, got into his Land Rover, and headed for the Blackthorn Antiquarian Museum. Upon arriving, he stopped at the main desk and saw Stephen Rawlings who had accepted the job as the museum's curator at Gallagher's urgings and has proven to very competent at his new job.

"Stephen, how are things going today?"

"Hi Gallagher...! The museum has been very busy. Several field trips from a number of schools in the valley have descended on us today. What brings you by today? I thought you were on some big investigation Anna told me about."

"I am and that's why I'm here. I believe we have a book containing the biography of Nathaniel Hawthorne."

Stephen looks at his latest inventory list and says, "It should be in aisle twenty under American Authors."

"Thanks. Do your parents miss you at the grocery store?"

"They do but Scott hired a friend of his to help out with stocking the shelves and some of the home deliveries. They are happy about my new job and so am I. I feel more cultured in this environment. I want to thank you again for the opportunity."

"What's family for but to help each other out?"

Gallagher then walked over to aisle twenty and found exactly what he was looking for right away. He turned to the page describing the Salem Athenaeum Library. It was founded in 1810. Gallagher then said goodbye to Stephen and headed back to Eagle House content on knowing what the next step should be.

***

7

Gallagher rose early the next morning and made his way downstairs to the kitchen where Anna was cooking up breakfast. "That smells so good? Is it what I think?"

"Your favorite, eggs sunny side up with bacon, corned beef hash and biscuits."

"Wow, and we are not even going on a hike this morning."

"Well who knows what we'll find in Salem. How long of a trip is it anyways?"

"It's about a hundred and thirty-two mile drive. It shouldn't take us longer than two and a half hours to get there."

"I know you mentioned it last night but I was a little tired. What exactly do you hope to find in Salem?"

"The Athenaeum Library was a regular hang out for Hawthorne. It's where he wrote much of his works. I am hoping to find any notes he may have jotted down when he wrote 'The Ambitious Guest'. A library like that keeps everything filed away for posterity sake."

'Knock Knock'

"Did I hear a knock on the door?" Anna asked.

"I'll see who it is." Gallagher said as he got up to answer the door.

"Jonathan, why the knock...? You usually come right in."

"Not at six in the morning now that you're a married man. I just wanted to catch you before you left for Salem. Chief Perry received the results from the jeweler. "The wedding ring is made of solid gold and is extremely old, dating back centuries. It was a very expensive ring for its time and its worth, because of its age and condition, could be worth millions now. The man in the cave was definitely no farmer to have had such a ring. He also said those four words engraved on the inside of the ring, 'Dieu et mon Droit' is the Coat of Arms of the King of England.""

"I know. It's old French meaning, 'God and My Right'"

"Well anyways, Perry said you can pick it up anytime because according to law, the statue of limitations ended many years ago; so finders keepers, isn't that great news? Talk about finding buried treasure."

"What am I going to do with someone else's gold wedding ring? I want to find out who the person was and if he has any family left living in the area; they should have it, not me. I do not care how much it's worth. I will keep it in my vault at the museum for now. In the meantime could you write an article in the Observer about finding a women's gold wedding ring on Mount Willey and if anyone knows who the owner could've been to come forward?"

Jonathan nods and says, "Sure. The Associated Press will pick up the story and it will go nationwide. Many families have come and gone throughout this valley since the Willey landslide. It will reach a much larger audience by having the AP carry the story. I will instruct them to come to the police station first so the museum won't get bombarded with possible gold diggers if you know what I mean."

"I can't imagine anyone living around here today knowing of such a person or his family, never mind nationwide, but it's worth a try."

"People keep family albums and pass them on to the next generation and so on. It's possible something might have been recorded in the newspaper or they may have old photos of their distant relatives."

Gallagher acknowledged the idea. "I seem to recall the first known photograph was taken sometime between 1826 and 1827 in France by Joseph Nicéphore Niépce. The chances of this man possessing a camera at that time, is quite remote."

"You said the first *known* photograph. I think if anyone back in 1826 could purchase a solid gold wedding ring, could probably have had access to the latest technology of the times and afford a camera."

Gallagher thinks for moment. "I think you may have shed more light on what I should look for in Salem."

"What's that?"

"The man found in the cave was obviously not a poor man like you're suggesting to have bought such an expensive ring."

"You mean he probably wasn't really a farmer from around here but he may have traveled some distance to get here?"

"That's my thinking, but who knows? We might find out there is more to this than just finding an expensive ring. We still do not know who the man was, or the woman, he was intending to marry. We also do not know why the words, were inscribed on the ring. Was the ring originally the property of a King?"

"Intended for a future Queen..." Jonathan added.

***

Gallagher and Anna left for Salem not knowing what to expect. The chances of finding what they were looking for was a long shot but it was the only shot they had. Two hours later, they pulled into the parking lot of the Salem Athenaeum Library. It was about one in the afternoon and the library was filling up with tourists, students and information hunters like themselves. They walked up to the receptionist who was sitting at her desk, "Good afternoon! My name is Gallagher Brady and this is my wife Anna. I am a bibliophile and the proprietor of the Blackthorn Antiquarian Museum in Jackson, New Hampshire. We are interested in researching any personal notes Nathaniel Hawthorne might have made during the time he wrote his short story, 'The Ambitious Guest'. I have learned this is where he penned the work."

The receptionist hesitates for a moment. "There's a section located in the William Bradford Room to your left marked Hawthorne, Holmes and Melville.

They were close friends and shared many of their ideas and thoughts with each other. I am sure you will find something there. Are you writing a book?"

"I neglected to mention it when I first introduced myself but I'm also a private investigator. I tend to leave that detail out because it's only necessity that forces me into that particular role."

"I see. Well I hope you find what you're looking for."

As soon as they left the lobby area, the receptionist went to her phone. The person on the other end answers and says, "Chester Peabody speaking."

"Chester, its Marie... I remember you telling me if anyone showed an unusual interest in Nathaniel Hawthorne's story, the Ambitious Guest to let you know. Well we have such a guest who is inquiring about the story and he claims to be an investigator from Jackson, New Hampshire.

"Thank you Marie. As you know Daren and I for several years now, have been wondering if Nathaniel's story would ever draw the attention of an investigator. The reason why we started working here back in the late forties was because of the connection our family had with Nathaniel."

"Am I being too inquisitive if I ask what's so interesting about the story of the Ambitious Guest?"

"If this gentleman is truly from Jackson, which is only a stone's throw from Crawford Notch; someone must have found something that is very

42

dear to my heart and to my family. I suppose there's no harm in telling you."

"Thank you Chester but if this is a private family matter I don't want to pry."

"Yes it's a family matter but I know you and Darin are serious about your feelings for each other so it's just a matter of time he would tell you everything before your future wedding."

"Wow! Now my interest has definitely peaked."

"Nathaniel inherited a gold ring from his father, Captain Nathaniel Hathorne. He was a sea captain and a member of the East India Marine Society and it is presumed he found the ring in the Falkland Islands after one of his sailing trips around Cape Horn. He decided to drop anchor on the island of East Falkland in 1799 to replenish supplies. While he was there he spent some time exploring the islands because it was thought there may be the remains of a treasure that was lost at sea back in 1795."

"Why do you say presumed...?"

"It's only presumed because we don't have any more definite information than that to go on. The ship which sank in 1795 was never made public and Hathorne never said publicly where he found the ring."

"You're right. It doesn't seem like much to go on."

"There's only this one possibility. The waters around Cape Horn are notorious for sinking ships. The natives on the island have a story they tell about finding the remains of a ship's cargo one morning in the year 1795 on some of the islands after a severe tropical storm. The cargo included several gold and silver coins. If you put the two together, it seems to fit. Hathorne died in 1808 of yellow fever in Suriname. In his last will and testament he left the ring to his son Nathaniel."

"What's so special about this gold ring and what does it have to do with the story?"

"From what I've been able to gather, Nathaniel had planned someday to offer the ring in marriage to my great aunt Sophia upon their engagement."

"So what happened?"

"The ring mysteriously went missing in 1824. Nathaniel and Sophia eventually did get married but not until 1842 and during that whole period of time the ring was never found or mentioned publicly by Nathaniel."

"I still don't see how the story of the Ambitious Guest fits into all this?"

"Another presumption on my part is, one of Nathaniel's schoolmates may have stolen the ring from him. In some of his private notes, which I found among his writings, he admitted being quite embarrassed about the loss of a ring because of its value and because it was the only thing, his father had left him. The story about the Ambitious Guest may have been a form of satire, which was a way for him to deal with his loss emotionally."

"Does the story mention the ring?"

"No, not directly but it describes an unnamed stranger who visits an Inn one night in Crawford

Notch and dines with the family who lived there. The stranger is a man of great ambition and self-worth. He wanted to make something of his life so a monument would be erected as a remembrance of him when he died and was buried. A young girl charmed by the stranger, described as a mountain nymph, infatuates the stranger. Before the love could ever blossom the stranger and the entire family died in a landslide that very night."

"This stranger, is it depicting Nathaniel himself?"

"No...I believe he was referring to the schoolmate who stole the ring."

"I see what you mean about it being a satire; a very sad one."

"What I'm wondering about is how this Mr. Brady has been able to connect the ring to this library. He must have come across some information my family had no knowledge of after all these years."

"Are you going to talk to him?"

"Most definitely but I need some time to do a little more investigating on my own. It should take them a few hours to sift through all those notes. I have a notebook, which contains bits of information that I have collected through the years since I have known about the missing ring. I need to review some of those notes before I come down and introduce myself. Can you bring me up some coffee; this might take a while."

"Yes Mr. Peabody, The library has quieted down at the moment. I'll be right up."

***

Gallagher and Anna started searching through several folders containing random notes on many of the stories from the collected works called, 'Twice-Told Tales'. After three tedious hours they came up dry. Gallagher put the folders back in the cabinet and showing his frustration said to Anna, "There's not one notation having to do with the 'Ambitious Guest'. There are notes on every other story but not that one. There is something fishy about this. It's the only story without notes."

"What are you thinking?"

"Someone doesn't want anyone else to know what those notes contained. We might as well go; there's nothing more we can find out here."

They were about to leave the library when they were stopped by the exit door. "Excuse me Mr. Brady. My name is Chester Peabody."

Gallagher is stunned at hearing the name. "Are you...."

"Yes I am. I'm a distant relation of Sophia Amelia Peabody who later married Nathaniel Hawthorne who would be my great uncle through marriage."

"I suppose you're wondering what my interest could be with Nathaniel's story."

"That's definitely an understatement but I have a pretty good idea considering the fact you are an investigator. I did some investigating of my own while you were looking through Hawthorne's notes. I know you are the respected bibliophile and private investigator. You are the one who broke up the Fifth Column organization in New Hampshire

46

about five years ago. I remember reading about it and I just brushed up on some newspaper articles I had filed away in my safe. You see, I've always been interested in that part of our country for a variety of reasons."

"Why...? Do you have some family connections there?"

"You could say that..."

"Can you tell me why there are no notes Hawthorne might have kept when he wrote the Ambitious Guest?" Gallagher asked perplexed. "All his other works have several notes."

"I can explain it to you in the privacy of my office."

Gallagher remained silent for a moment while looking at Anna. "We would like to stay and talk with you if you have the time. We have found something that has led us here."

"I'm making the time. You may have the missing pieces of a puzzle my brother and I have been trying to piece together for several years now."

"My good friend and partner in my investigations is a freelance reporter for the Jackson Observer. He has taken the liberty to place an article in the latest edition describing what we have found, which should be hitting the newsstands as we speak."

A grave look came over Peabody's face. "I wish it would've been kept out of the papers. It could cause an interest to those of an unsavory sort."

"I see by your reaction you have some idea what we may have found."

"I'm guessing you found a gold wedding ring. If it is the ring as I suspect it is, it was intended to given to my great aunt Sophia upon her engagement to Nathaniel. We have no tangible proof the ring belonged to Nathaniel. The knowledge of the rings existence was never been made public by Nathaniel for various reasons but he did describe the ring in his private notes. His future wife Sophia was never told of its existence, even though she was the intended receiver of the ring upon their engagement."

"That explains why we didn't find any notes," Gallagher said. "Why do you think the ring we found is the same ring?"

"A little over five years ago I wrote an article in our local paper, which is syndicated nationwide, stating the loss of a gold wedding ring somewhere in the Crawford Notch area of New Hampshire back in the early eighteen hundreds. I said the ring's value was not the reason for my interest but it was for sentimental reasons because it was a family treasure. I offered twenty-five thousand dollars reward to the individual who ever found it. Shortly after I wrote the article, I received an anonymous hand written letter threatening me to stop looking or inquiring about the ring. It stated clearly the ring did not belong to my family."

"What else did Nathaniel's notes reveal?"

"Please come up to my office. I will show you what I've collected so far." Peabody then directs his attention to Marie. "Marie it's getting close to closing time; call it a day. I will lock up. I will be up in my office for a while. What I was talking to you about earlier is exactly why Mr. Brady has come here today."

After Marie said goodbye Anna and Gallagher followed Peabody upstairs then suddenly at the top of the stairs right before entering his office, Peabody began clutching his left harm and quickly dropped to the floor with a gasp. Anna rushed to his side and felt for a pulse. She looked at Gallagher, "He's not breathing!"

Gallagher bent down and touched the side of his neck. "Anna, call for an ambulance! I'll try to resuscitate him. He either has suffered a heart attack or stroke."

After about two minutes Gallagher looked at Anna and said, "He's starting to breath."

The ambulance should be here in five minutes," Anna said.

Gallagher started looking around the room to see if he could figure out what Peabody was about to show them. After a careful search around the room, his eyes fell upon a large wall safe. Gallagher tries pulling on the handle and to his surprise; the door was slightly ajar. He then looks at Anna and says, "What he was about to show us may be in this safe."

Anna shakes her head. "The ambulance and a police cruiser just arrived. I think you better hold up for awhile until they leave."

"We may have to leave when they do. I have to take my chances and quickly look inside."

Anna runs to the top of the stairs. "They are coming through the front door right now. Hurry...!"

Gallagher quickly sorts through some loose papers and then finds a notebook. He grabs it, quickly flips through the pages, and then puts it in his coat pocket just in time before the police reach the top of the stairs. He looks at Anna and nods his head.

Anna directs the officer and the medical team to the entrance of Peabody's office where he is lying on the floor just where he had fallen. The medical team worked on Peabody and was able to stabilize him. One of the medical technicians looks at Gallagher. "He has suffered a severe stroke and he needs to be taken to the hospital immediately."

One of the police officers who arrived with the medical team looked at Gallagher puzzled, "I've never seen you around here before. Peabody normally doesn't invite visitors to his office, are you friends or family?"

"No, we never met him before. My wife and I are doing some research and we came here with the hopes of collecting some information. Mr. Peabody kindly invited us to his office to show us something that would help in our research and as soon as we walked in here he suddenly collapsed."

"Who are you? What's your name?"

"My name is Gallagher Brady and this is my wife Anna."

"Where are you from?"

Gallagher was starting to get annoyed with all the questions and revealing his irritation replies in a curt manner, "Excuse me officer; you seem to be more interested in who we are and where we come from than in what happened to Mr. Peabody."

The officer eased off with his questions and replied apologetically, "I'm sorry if I've been quick with the questions. Mr. Peabody has had threats made on his life recently and we are just being overly cautious. We already ran your plates when you pulled into the parking lot. That's how cautious we have become around here. We know who you are and please except my apologize Mr. Brady and...."

"Yes...I'm Mrs. Brady; the one who called for the ambulance."

"Any clues to whose been threatening him?" Gallagher asked.

"Not yet. Whoever is doing it is very good at keeping a low profile because as you can see we watch this place very well."

"How do the threats come?"

"After the original threat came by letter it was always by a hand written note found in the library's mailbox. The mailbox is in front of the building and can easily be seen from the street. Our police station is directly across from the library and we have a twenty-four hour surveillance camera monitoring the entrance including the mailbox. Peabody requested the camera after he started receiving the threats."

"Is the mailbox the type that can be locked?"

"Yes, it can only be accessed by the mail carrier. It does not even have a slot for outgoing mail so no one can slip anything inside. The carrier has to come inside to pick any outgoing mail. Chester, his brother Daren and Marie are the only ones who have a key."

"Do you mind if I write some of this down?" Gallagher asked.

"Go right ahead. We've heard about your abilities and welcome any help you can give us."

"What do the notes he's been getting say?"

"The ring does not belong to you. If you pursue your search for the ring it could mean your life."

Gallagher thinks for a moment. How long has Marie been employed by the Peabody's?"

"Marie was hired about five years ago and the Peabody's have given her carte blanche in all the operations of the library. They trust her like family. As a matter-of fact Marie and Daren are planning to get married."

"Does Daren usually work here with Chester? The reason why I ask is because we haven't had a chance to meet him."

"He's only here between his trips abroad. He's the library's book collector and he travels to England and Europe several times a year. He has a passion for England. He actually attended Cambridge University for his post graduate studies."

"I'm familiar with the kind work he does. I am the proprietor of the Blackthorn Antiquarian Library in

Jackson, New Hampshire. I also have an affinity to England. I lived there for fourteen years and attended Oxford University before returning to where I was born in Jackson."

"We know because when we ran your plates your profile came up and listed you as a bibliophile and to our surprise, a private investigator."

"The latter is the reason why I'm here today."

"What are you investigating, if I may ask?"

Gallagher smiles, "The original owner of the ring."

"You mean the ring that Chester has been warned not to search for?"

"The very same one...."

***

8

After Gallagher gave the officer more of his personal information in case there were any more questions, they left the library. Gallagher asked Anna to drive while he took out the small leather book from his pocket. Anna sees the book. "How come you kept the book?"

"I really had no choice. I had to hide it in my coat pocket and I did not have the chance to put it back because we all left Peabody's office at the same time. What was I supposed to do; admit I raided his safe?"

Gallagher begins flipping through the book and at first glance, he sees nothing that catches his eye

53

except a small piece of paper folded inside the book. "We'll have to study it when we get back to Jackson. It looks like it's filled with Chester's notes."

***

Two hours later, they arrived at Eagle House and noticed a cruiser parked in the driveway. "Looks like the Chief is paying us a visit," exclaimed Gallagher as he gets out of his car.

They both walked into the living room and saw Chief Perry talking with his Aunt Helen and her husband Bill. "Am I missing something important?" Gallagher asked as he joined them.

Tom Perry nods and says, "We got a call about an hour ago from the Salem Police. After you left, they called Marie at her home and told her what happened. Shortly after that, they caught her snooping around Mr. Peabody's office after the police had cordoned it off until they complete their investigation. The police arrested her and is being held at the police station because she refuses to tell them why she entered his office. They are waiting for the forensic report on the cause of Peabody's death. Until then everyone who was in the library at the time of his death is under suspicion. That includes you and Anna."

Gallagher is puzzled by the development and says, "This Marie is engaged to Chester Peabody's brother Daren. Why is she being held on suspicion?"

"Your guess is as good as mine."

Anna looks at Gallagher. "I'm surprised she was able to get by the surveillance camera without being noticed."

"Well that's the funny thing," Tom declared. "When she returned to the library, the police watched and allowed her to enter the library even though they had already marked it as a crime scene."

Anna shakes her head. "Why are they calling it a crime scene? We were there when he collapsed; there was no foul play involved."

Gallagher nods. "Clever move; it allowed them time to see why she went back to the library and I think I know why."

"You know it means you can't leave the country," Tom said with a grin.

Gallagher laughs. "I wouldn't think of it. We have a very interesting set of circumstances surrounding the death of Peabody, the body found in the cave and the ring; not to mention Hawthorne's Ambitious Guest and now this Marie, the mystery woman."

Helen perks up and says, "What did you find out while you were there?"

Gallagher sits beside Anna. "It seems this Chester Peabody along with his younger Daren, who we never met, was hoping someone would show up some day inquiring about the ring. He said they have been waiting for several years for someone to find it. He was about to show us something in his office when he collapsed to the floor."

Gallagher then pulls the notebook out of his coat pocket. "After I got him breathing again and waiting for the ambulance to arrive I looked around his office and noticed a wall safe. I tried the door handle to see if it was unlocked and to my surprise, it was partially open. He may have been looking for something right before he met us in the lobby when we were about to leave and I think it was this notebook."

Chief Perry looks at the book in Gallagher's hand and says while shaking his head, "I don't want to see it. I'm going to ignore what you did but if they find out you took it; you will have a lot to answer for and you are probably looking at an arrest on the charge of breaking and entering his safe and it could implicate you in his death until an autopsy rules out foul play."

Gallagher nods and says, "My guess is the only ones who may know of the notebooks existence is Peabody's brother and possibly Marie who's now in jail. It may very well be why she went back to his office."

"There's no way of finding out without you admitting you took the book," Perry said.

"I know. I have to think about this."

Helen speaks up and says to Chief Perry, "You want some coffee? This could take a while."

Chief Perry accepts Helen's offer and is about to step into the kitchen when Officer Taylor enters the room and says, "Chief, you just got a call from Salem's Chief of Police. He said it is very urgent. He gave me this number and you can call him direct; he's waiting for your call."

Perry goes to the phone in Gallagher's study and dials. "Chief Johnson here," said a voice on the other end. "Is this Chief Perry?"

"Yes Chief. Do you have some news?"

"Tell Mr. Brady the woman named Marie has been released from custody."

"Why?"

"We got a call from the British Embassy in Washington demanding her release immediately. She's apparently working undercover for the British Government and has diplomatic immunity."

"Where do we go from here?"

"Tell Mr. Brady he has our full cooperation in helping him find what this is all about. Our hands are tied because of this latest development and so are yours but Mr. Brady's hands are not."

"He's right here. Do you want to tell him yourself?"

"Put him on."

Perry hands the phone to Gallagher. "Chief, this is Gallagher Brady."

"Mr. Brady. Pursue your investigation. You may have stumbled on to something bigger than we are. I can't imagine why the British government is involved in all this."

"I think I may have some idea," Gallagher replied.

"Care to share it?"

"Let me put it to you this way. The ring we were inquiring about with Chester Peabody may have belonged at one time to a King."

"What King?"

"The King of England."

"Well like I said before, it's out of our hands. As soon as we get the results from the medical examiner on cause of death I will pass it on to you."

"I'm not very happy about how this has evolved but I guess I'm in it for the long haul."

"Thanks Mr. Brady. I have your contact information you gave us before you left Salem. Is it okay to reach you at that number?"

"Yes...I've been meaning to get a special red phone but it will have to do."

"What?"

"Never mind Chief; it's a private joke. I will let you know of my progress. There will be a partner of mine named Jonathan Henry who will be on the case with me."

"I know the name from the two previous cases you were involved in and you will have our complete cooperation."

"Thanks Chief. I will be in touch."

"Oh, one more thing you should know. We have been trying to locate Darin Peabody to let him know what happened to Chester but all the numbers we had on file are no longer in service.

We are looking into it as I speak. I will keep you updated."

'Click'

***

9

After Chief Perry left Eagle House, Gallagher and Anna immediately went into their study and began looking through the notebook.

"Maybe you should call Jonathan," Anna said after thinking about what this could all mean.

"Are you jumping ship just as it's starting to get interesting?"

"You may think it's interesting but once I heard we are dealing with the embassy of another country, all I can think about is foreign spies."

"I think you may be right. I would rather you go back to overseeing things at the Turning Page while Jonathan and I get further involved in this investigation. Kathy has been running the show at the bookshop for the past few days and she could use a break."

"That's a great idea. I'm glad you understand. So what are going to do next?"

"I think the best place to start is finding out more about the ring and where it came from."

"Where do you start?"

"This notebook..."

***

Jonathan arrived at Eagle House later that evening and he brought with him as much as he could find on the two families that had disappeared from the Notch right after the Willey landslide.

"I looked through all these news clippings having to do with the landslide and events that took place shortly thereafter it but I didn't find anything of substance that can help us," Jonathan declared revealing his frustration.

"There has to be some connection with my great grandfather's unnamed schoolmate, who traveled sixty-six miles in a horse drawn carriage on a day that had threatening weather brewing on the horizon, and one of those families in Crawford Notch; if not both. The woman, his fiancée, may have come from one of those families."

Gallagher pulls out the notebook. "The answer must lie somewhere in the pages of this book."

Later that night Gallagher finished reading through the entire notebook and then dropped it off to Jonathan for him to study. Gallagher told Jonathan of his plans for the following day and retired for the night with a million thoughts running through his head.

**

10

The following morning Gallagher got up at dawn and drove to the Village Tavern for a hearty breakfast before driving to Bowdoin College in

Maine to find out what he could about the graduating class of 1825.

Gus and Lars Swenson were busy in the kitchen preparing breakfast for the early birds when Gallagher entered through the back door as he usually does.

Gus Swenson, with his big smile says, "God middag Gallagher! What brings you by so early this morning?"

"Good morning Gus and good morning Lars. I have about an hour drive ahead of me this morning and I didn't want to wake up Anna to make my breakfast so I'm here ready for a plate of your Belgian waffles and a cup of your supercharged black coffee; I think I'm going to need it."

"Where are you going?" Lars asked in his usual inquisitive way.

"Bowdoin College in Maine... I have to find out who were the classmates of my great grandfather, Graham Blackthorn, back in the early eighteen hundreds. I'm hoping they had kept records back that far."

Lars perks up and says, "That's odd! A woman was in here yesterday asking if we knew the Blackthorn family."

"What did she look like?" Gallagher asked surprised.

"She was very attractive, in her mid-thirties with long dark hair and dark brown eyes. She looked like she was here on business the way she was dressed. She was carrying a briefcase and was driving a very expensive car. It looked like a late model Mercedes Benz."

Gallagher shakes his head and says, "Lars, you ought to be an investigator yourself. You have her described right down to her birthmark."

Lars blushes and says, "I must admit she was gorgeous; I couldn't take my eyes off her."

"You said she was inquiring about my family. What did you tell her?"

Lars smiles and says, "You will be proud of me. I said there were no more Blackthorns left in the valley, which when you think about it, since you changed your name and Helen married Bill Waters there are no more Blackthorns in the valley. I wasn't about to tell her anything about your family especially with what I overheard Chief Perry saying to officer Taylor who was in here not long before she showed up."

"What did you overhear?"

Just as Lars was going to answer, Jonathan walked in through the back door and spots Gallagher. "I'm glad you didn't leave yet. I called your house and Anna said you had already left for Maine. She said you left without having breakfast so I came right here knowing you as I do."

"Did you find out something?"

"Oh yeah...I found out something alright. I decided to look through the notebook you gave me last night and I found a section in there about a ship sinking off the South American coast near Cape Horn."

"Yeah, I remember reading it and it did catch my attention. What about it?"

"Well I decided to call the Observer last night and one of my colleagues was working the nightshift in the archive room and I asked him if there was anything recorded about a sailing ship sinking off the coast of Cape Horn back during the seventeenth or eighteenth centuries. He called me back about an hour later and told me back in 1795 a British warship carrying an enormous treasure, belonging to King George of England, sank about sixty nautical miles off the coast of Cape Horn. It was on its way to the Falklands for safekeeping because of the ongoing war with France. The treasure was confiscated in battle by a Spanish warship, which later sank after being caught is a major storm off the coast of the Falkland Islands."

Gallagher's eyes lit up after hearing Jonathan's account. "The gold ring we found in the cave; it must have come from King George's treasure. That explains the inscription on the ring; it all connects."

"Everything seems to be pointing in that direction. Let's think about what we have found out so far."

Gallagher looks at Lars. "Can you get me a pen and paper? I need to write all this down."

Gallagher and Jonathan sat down at a table in a far corner of the Tavern for privacy and started listing everything they knew so far. First, they found an unknown dead man in a cave in the approximate area where the Willey landslide occurred back in 1826 killing the entire family. The dead man was in possession of a gold wedding ring. Nathaniel

63

Hawthorne had written a short story some twenty-one years later about an unnamed person he called the 'ambitious guest' who visits an Inn located in Crawford Notch on the very same night of the infamous Willey landslide. In the story, the unnamed person dies in the landslide along with the entire Willey family. According to my great grandfather's journal, an unnamed schoolmate graduated with Hawthorne and my great grandfather in the same year from Bowdoin College. This unnamed schoolmate was planning to travel to Crawford Notch to propose to his fiancé on the very same night of the Willey landslide. The evidence found in the journal leads us to the Athenaeum Library in Salem, Massachusetts where Hawthorne wrote the 'Ambitious Guest'. After arriving at the library Anna and I meet Chester Peabody, a distant relative of Sophia Peabody who was Nathaniel Hawthorne's wife. He suddenly collapses before he is able to show us something in his office. Gallagher finds a small notebook in Peabody's safe and took it before the police showed up thinking it may be what he was going to show us. A few hours later, Peabody's receptionist named Marie was snooping around in his office after the police cordoned it off. They arrested her and took her to jail. Shortly thereafter, the British Embassy releases her because she has diplomatic immunity.

Gallagher suddenly jumps up from his table, goes into the kitchen to finds Lars and asks, "What did you overhear Perry tell Taylor?"

"He believes there are spies in the valley."

"If the woman driving the Mercedes shows up here again, call me or Jonathan as soon as you can."

***

11

Gallagher took the notebook from Jonathan and left the Village Tavern thinking all kinds of things after hearing that spies may be somewhere in the valley. The description of the woman Lars was referring to did not match the woman named Marie he had met in Salem. What reason could there be for foreign spies to be asking questions about his family? Did it have something to do with his great grandfather? Did it have to do with the man found in the cave who possessed the gold ring? Did the ring originally belong to King George the Third of England?

***

Gallagher drove southeast on Rte. 302 then turned onto Rte. 95 north and headed for Brunswick Maine. As he was driving, he noticed a black Mercedes had been tailing him for the past seventy miles. The scene reminded him of the time he and Jonathan were leaving the town of Lincoln one night five years ago and had to outwit the pursuer. What made it possible to outwit them was because it was at night. This time it is in broad daylight. Gallagher decided not to panic and just proceeded to drive to Bowdoin College and take his chances.

***

Meanwhile Jonathan decided to follow-up on finding more information about the two families that left the Crawford Notch area right after the tragedy. He pulls into the Trading Post in Harts Location hoping to see Daisy Saffron and find out more about the families.

"Jonathan, it's so good to see you!" exclaimed Daisy as Jonathan walked through the front door. "Are you involved in the same investigation as Gallagher?"

"Yes I am."

"Well I'm glad you came by because I just got to thinking about the two families that mysteriously left after the Willey landslide and I found out a little more information that may help."

"I was hoping you did. What did you find out?"

"One of the families was named Erickson. They owned the Erickson Farm, which was located directly in the path of the landslide. They lost all their livestock. It ruined them financially. According to my sources, they left in a hurry because they owed several hundred dollars to an unknown lender. Being unable to pay him back, they left with just the clothes on their backs."

"Did they have a daughter?"

"No, they had two sons."

"Okay, that takes care of one family; how about the other?"

"The only bit of information I could get was they had a daughter about twenty-two years old. She had left for Boston early in the morning the day before the landslide and sailed to Europe with plans to never to return to the Notch. It is rumored she suffered a broken heart. Her parents were never seen after the slide and they were never heard from again."

"Now that's mysterious. Were you able to find out their names?"

"There are no records of the family's name. That's mysterious in itself."

"It sure is. Well Daisy, you have been a great help. You found out more than our own police department. I see all those mystery novels you read have made you quite the detective."

Daisy reveals her big toothless smile and says, "Thanks Jonathan. I've always wanted to be like Nora Charles in the Thin Man series."

Jonathan laughs and says, "I think you really want to be like Myrna Loy."

Daisy returns a laugh and says, "I guess I can't fool you."

***

Gallagher is walking towards the entrance of the college and hears a voice call out to him from behind. He turns around and sees a woman matching Lars description approach him. "Excuse me Mr. Brady but can I talk with you?"

"You have me at a loss. Do I know you?"

"No...we've never met before but I know who you are and what you found."

"I don't understand."

"Can we sit and talk?"

Gallagher looks at his watch. "Sure, I'll make the time."

"Can we go somewhere private?"

"We can go inside the school. It looks like they have a lobby just inside the entrance. It doesn't look very busy right now."

"No...that wouldn't be a good choice." She points across the street. "How about over there at that coffee shop?"

"Okay."

Gallagher remains silent as they make their way to the coffee shop. As they are walking Gallagher notices, the woman keeps looking around as though she expected someone else to show up. He decides to remain silent. They enter the shop and find a quiet spot in a far corner.

Before Gallagher sits he asks, "What's this all about. You follow me the entire trip from Jackson and you were the woman asking questions about my family in the Village Tavern. Who are you?"

"My name is Jessica Williams and I need to talk to you about the gold wedding ring you found on Mount Willey. I read about it in the newspaper and it said the ring is at the Jackson Police Department for anyone to claim. I went there to see it but the desk clerk said I would have to talk with you first."

"What is it about this ring that interests you?"

Jessica swallows. "It was an engagement ring intended to be offered to my great grandmother by her fiancé."

Gallagher stunned by her statement. "How do you know this?"

"I found a letter in my grandmother's personal things after she died; it was in her family Bible. The letter was addressed to my mother. In the letter it stated that my great grandmother, Elizabeth Adams, was to have received a gold engagement ring on the night of August 28th 1826 from her fiancé, a Mr. John Browning."

"Who sent the letter to your great grandmother?"

"Graham Blackthorn, your great grandfather."

Gallagher got up from the table and walked away for a moment trying to grasp what he had just heard.

"Are you alright?" Jessica asked with genuine concern in her voice.

Gallagher sat back down and took out the notebook from his pocket and from the middle of it he pulled out a folded piece of paper. He hands it to Jessica and says, "You might want to read this."

She takes it and begins reading it in a low voice;

On March 20, 1824, an unknown thief stole a gold ring belonging to Nathanial Hawthorne. The rings intended recipient was his future wife, Sophia Amelia Peabody. Nathaniel suspected a schoolmate of his had stolen the ring but was never revealed by Hawthorne and was never spoken of in public.

She looked at Gallagher after reading it. "Is this saying my great grandmother's intended husband was a thief?"

"What other meaning can you get from those words?"

Gallagher then looks out the window and stares at the front entrance to the college. "I guess there's no need for me to find out more about Hawthorne's schoolmate, because according to your great grandmother's letter his name was John Browning. Speaking of that; what was your great grandmother's maiden name again?"

"Elizabeth Adams."

"She must have eventually found someone else and got married because you're living proof."

She nods. "Yes, after she realized John wasn't coming back to mend their relationship after they had had a big argument over setting a date for their wedding she left Crawford Notch right after the Willey landslide. The slide destroyed most of her family's property and they did not have the resources to rebuild. She had suffered a broken heart and never wanted to go back to the Notch and left for Europe. In time she finally found a man she could love and settled down with and eventually they moved to California."

Gallagher just shakes his head. "All that time she never knew John had traveled most of that day and night with the threat of bad weather on the horizon to see her and ask for her hand in marriage."

"Yes...I'm afraid that's the sad truth."

"Sad truth is right. What's even sadder is we found John Browning's body in a cave on Mount Willey."

"It's what I was afraid of hearing. My great grandmother never left word where she was moving to when she left for Europe so your great grandfather may have tried to reach her somehow and tell her. However, back in those days it was hard to track people down; not like today. In time my parents moved back East after my grandparents died and they settled in Moultonborough on Lake Winnipesaukee."

"Oh...we're just about neighbors."

"That's right and once I found out about what happened to my great grandmother I've always been interested in finding out exactly what happened on that night. Mr. Henry's article about finding a gold wedding ring immediately caught my attention."

"Sentimental reasons I imagine."

"Of course but I guess it's all for nothing. It appears the ring is really stolen property and rightfully belongs to the Peabody family."

"Not so fast. According this notebook, which was the property of the late Chester Peabody who was a distant relation to Nathaniel Hawthorne's wife

Sophia, Hawthorne's father discovered the gold ring in the Falkland Islands who was a sea captain back in 1799. My associate Jonathan Henry has been doing some research and found out the ring was part of a much larger treasure belonging to King George the Third of England. During a battle with a Spanish warship in the south Atlantic back in 1795, the treasure was confiscated. The Spanish ship eventually sank off the coast of the Falklands losing an enormous treasure to the sea."

"Are you serious?"

"Why would I make up something like that?"

"It seems so unbelievable?"

"Well let me tell you something you may not be aware of; we think there are foreign spies trying to get their hands on the ring."

"What's so special about the ring that would interest foreign spies?"

"I believe it has something to do with the inscription on the inside of the ring."

"Do you know that for certain?"

"We know of a woman who has been working undercover at the Athenaeum Library in Salem, Massachusetts for the past five years. She may be working for the British government because she has diplomatic clearance. Mr. Chester Peabody, the curator of the library, hired her to work as a receptionist. Peabody was a distant relation of Sophia Amelia Peabody, the wife of Nathaniel Hawthorne as I mentioned earlier. Peabody possessed this notebook, which he had kept inside his wall safe that contains information about the missing ring and much more. She was caught breaking into Peabody's office after it was cordoned off by the police and was taken away in cuffs only to be released shortly after she made her one phone call to the British Embassy because of her diplomatic immunity."

"This is getting more bizarre by the minute. Why in the world would the British government want a gold wedding ring?"

"Right now all we have to go on is the words that are inscribed on the ring."

"What does it say?"

"I apologize for leaning on the side of caution but its better if you don't know what it says for now. If we are dealing with foreign agents, they are not ones to mess with. I'm only thinking of your safety."

"I guess my gut feeling was correct."

"What do you mean?"

"I've had a feeling for some time that I'm being followed. That's why I wanted to speak to you in a private location."

"How long have you felt this way?"

"Several years ago I wrote a small piece in Life magazine about my great grandmother. It was a human-interest story that the publisher of the magazine thought should be in print. My father was a freelance writer for the magazine and he told him about my interest in having people know about what happened to my great grandmother; you know the typical heart wrenching tragic love story women love to read about. It was right after the magazine came out that I started suspecting I was being followed."

"Did you ever tell anyone?"

"No I didn't because I convinced myself it was only my imagination. But ever since the article Mr. Henry wrote in the newspaper my suspicions have become stronger."

Gallagher looks at his watch and says, "I must be getting back to Jackson. The rest of my life is waiting for me. We must talk again. How can I reach you if I find out more?"

"Here's my card. I live in San Diego now but my family still owns the cottage on Lake Winnipesaukee. I spend a few weeks there during the summer and the fall. My address and phone number are on this card. I will not be going back to my home in San Diego for at least another month or two. I love this time of year in the mountains."

Gallagher takes it and without saying, another word gets into his Land Rover and starts driving away. As he is driving he looks in his review mirror and notices Jessica getting into her Mercedes and starts to follow him instead of going in the direction of the lake. She continues following him all the way back to Jackson; almost to his driveway at Eagle House then drives on by. He begins to wonder why she took the route back to Jackson when Lake Winnipesaukee was in the opposite direction.

***

Later that night, Gallagher began studying the words that were inscribed on the ring with his magnifying glass. The significance of the words was a troubling twist after Gallagher learned that John Browning and Elizabeth Adams were the couple tragically separated by a silly argument and the Willey landslide. Did John Browning actually steal the ring from Hawthorne, and if he did, why? In addition, why are there foreign spies interested in the ring? Whom did it rightfully belong? Was it from King George's personal treasure?

Gallagher could not think anymore about it without his head spinning and decided to call it a night. Anna was still awake reading a book when he entered the bedroom. "You're still awake?"

"I decided to read the complete story of the Ambitious Guest for myself. I am trying to find out if there are any clues Hawthorne may have inserted in the story. So far I've come up dry."

Gallagher looks out the window and sees the full moon glistening like a glowing pearl surrounded by tiny diamonds. "The sky is clear tonight. I wish this mystery was as clear."

Anna laughs and says, "It wouldn't be a mystery then, would it?"

Gallagher smiles at her and says as he joins her in bed, "Maybe tomorrow something will come to light."

"Do you believe Jessica's story?"

"I'm not sure. She did not go home after we left Bowdoin. She must be staying up here for some reason. I will call Jonathan in the morning and have him trace down the person named Elizabeth Adams, who was her great grandmother."

"You don't believe she could be a spy?"

"If she is, she's a real good actress."

"Isn't that one of their signatures, a good disguise to fool the enemy?"

Gallagher picked up the book she was reading and starts looking through the pages.

"What are you doing? I thought you knew the story."

"Oh I do. I was just making sure you were reading Hawthorne and not one of Ian Fleming's novels."

They both kissed each other goodnight.

***

12

Gallagher woke up early the next morning with more questions on his mind than answers. The biggest question, which he wanted to clear up first was, why were there spies interested in the ring? If the ring was part of a much larger treasure that floated to the bottom of the south Atlantic when the Spanish ship was sunk and then hidden somewhere in the Falklands; did anyone have any real claim to the King's treasure after all these years except maybe treasure hunters? Gallagher decided to go down to the Blackthorn Antiquarian

Museum after breakfast. A little research was needed to answer that question.

The doors of the museum opened to the public at nine in the morning. Several people were standing by the front door when he arrived. Gallagher looked at his watch and it was five minutes to nine. He spoke to the gathering crowd. "I guess its close enough to nine friends. Please come in and enjoy your visit.

Gallagher walked through the main lobby of the two-story building and found Stephen Rawlings busy at his desk. "Good morning Stephen. What's the good word for the day?"

"Good morning Gallagher. I'm very happy to see you this morning." Stephen then pointed to a man sitting at the far side of the lobby. "You might want to talk with that gentleman over there by the window. He said it was urgent that he talk with you. He came by yesterday looking for you but I told him you were involved in a local matter and I was not sure when you would be here. He said he would be at the front door at first light this morning so he wouldn't miss you. I think you better talk with him. I can't imagine what could be so urgent."

Gallagher walked over to the young man who looked like he could be in his early thirties. "Hello... I'm Gallagher Brady. I was told you needed to talk with me."

The man looked at Gallagher for a few seconds before speaking. "Mr. Brady...my name is David Browning."

Gallagher gave him a double take after hearing his name. "Are you here for the reason I think you are?"

"I'm not quite sure. I live in the town of Raymond, not too far from here. I heard someone found a gold wedding ring on Mount Willey along with the body of a dead man. My great uncle, John Browning may have been that man."

Gallagher avoided showing any surprise. "Please come into my office. I'm anxious to hear why you believe we found your great uncle."

They entered Gallagher's office and shut the door. "Pardon my being over cautious but what we are about to talk about must remain in this room. Please tell me more about your great uncle."

"Where should I begin?"

"Try the beginning."

David appears to hesitate for moment.... "My great uncle John attended Bowdoin College during the same time as the famous author Nathaniel Hawthorne. They were close friends, which was unusual for Hawthorne to befriend someone outside the writers circle but they had much in common outside the literary world. Uncle John was a transcendentalist. Transcendentalists believe that society and its institutions, particularly organized religion and political parties; ultimately corrupt the purity of the individual. They have faith that people are at their best when truly "self-reliant" and independent. It is only from such real individuals that true community could be formed."

Gallagher nods and says, "I'm well informed of the movement. Ralph Waldo Emerson, Henry David Thoreau and many others of that time fostered those ideas."

"Your reputation of being a well read man precedes you. I've followed your recent exploits here in the valley and your philanthropic work, which I've been told is a family trait."

"Enough about me; please continue. I find what you are telling me about your uncle to be fascinating."

"As I was saying, they were close friends. They were so close because of their shared philosophy they would often share their most intimate thoughts and feelings about matters. One of them was the love my uncle had for a woman named Elizabeth Adams. Their relationship was for the most part the ideal romantic experience with many long walks on the beach, dinners by candlelight and a constant flow of gifts to each other but during that wonderful time the relationship would sometimes get strained emotionally. My uncle would often seek advice from Nathaniel when these times would arise."

Gallagher raised his hand gesturing David to stop for a moment. "How do you know about all these personal details?"

"My uncle kept a detailed diary. When my family finally realized he was missing they searched his home and found it. They read it to see if they could find out any information that would tell of his whereabouts. The last notation was dated August

15, 1826. He described a disagreement he recently had with Elizabeth. I guess my great uncle was dragging his feet when it came to asking for her hand in marriage. The courtship, in her opinion, was going on for much too long. It was a silly quarrel as they often were but both being very headstrong would not budge and give in to the other on this last episode, which turned into their final one. He mentioned he had a gold wedding ring, which he planned to give to her when he proposed to her. "

"Did he say where he got the ring?"

"There's no mention of it but he said something to the effect, and I quote, "It was a great sacrifice on my part but my love for you is worth more than the loss of any other friend I could have in this world."

"Do you know the friend he was referring to?"

"No,… it doesn't mention the friend or where he got the ring."

Gallagher took a deep breath. "We are sure we found your great uncle John because he was holding onto a leather pouch with the wedding ring inside. According to our medical examiner, he was about the age your uncle would have been in 1826. We have no other proof other than the fact he possessed the ring and the details of another story that matches yours."

"What story would that be?"

"Until I find out who else is interested in this ring I must keep their identity confidential for now."

"I understand. Do you have knowledge of any other interested parties?"

In light of the fact the ring has the interest of foreign spies, Gallagher scratched his head trying to come up with a delicate way of telling David what his involvement could mean.

"Anytime news of something valuable being found, it naturally always brings out the treasure hunters."

"I know what you mean. I assure you my interest in the ring is purely sentimental for my family's sake."

"I'm sure it is."

David left the library after realizing he was not going to sway Gallagher into revealing anything more. Gallagher went to the window and saw David driving off in a late model red Ferrari.

***

13

Gallagher left the museum and drove to the Turning Page Bookshop where Anna had already opened up for business.

"I was wondering when you would get here." Anna declared. "Tobey and the other children are waiting for you in the reading room; remember its Saturday morning."

Gallagher looked at his watch. "Time does go by and away we fly."

"What?"

"Psalm ninety, verse ten."

"Oh! I knew it had to have some intellectual meaning coming from you. What are you reading to the group today?"

"I thought I would read the Ambitious Guest."

"How appropriate…."

Gallagher entered the reading room and his audience was quiet and eager to hear Gallagher's narration of his selected story.

"Tobey Jones speaks up and asks, "What story do you have for us today?"

"Well kids I thought I would read you a story by Nathaniel Hawthorne called the Ambitious Guest."

They remained quiet and alert as Gallagher began reading…

'One September night a family had gathered round their hearth, and piled it high with the driftwood of mountain streams, the dry cones of the pine, and the splintered ruins of great trees that had come crashing down the precipice. Up the chimney roared the fire, and brightened the room with its broad blaze. The faces of the father and mother had a sober gladness; the children laughed; the eldest daughter was the image of Happiness at seventeen; and the aged grandmother, who sat knitting in the warmest place, was the image of Happiness grown old. They had found the "herb, heart's-ease," in the bleakest spot of all New England. This family were situated in the Notch of the White Hills, where the wind was sharp throughout the year, and pitilessly cold in the winter--giving their cottage all its fresh inclemency before it descended on the valley of the Saco. They dwelt in a cold spot and a dangerous one; for a mountain towered above their heads, so steep,* *that the stones would often rumble down its sides and startle them at midnight.'*

Indicated by their silence, the children seemed mesmerized by the story so Gallagher read on for several more minutes. Then when Gallagher came to the part describing the guest in more detail, it triggered something in his brain...

'The secret of the young man's character was a high and abstracted ambition. He could have borne to live an undistinguished life, but not to be forgotten in the grave. Yearning desire had been transformed to hope; and hope, long cherished, had become like certainty, that, obscurely as he journeyed now, a glory was to beam on all his pathway-though not, perhaps, while he was treading it. But when posterity should gaze back into the gloom of what was now the present, they would trace the brightness of his footsteps, brightening as meaner glories faded, and confess that a gifted one had passed from his cradle to his tomb with none to recognize him.

"As yet," cried the stranger, his cheek glowing and his eye flashing with enthusiasm, "As yet, I have done nothing. Were I to vanish from the earth tomorrow, none would know so much of me as you: that a nameless youth came up at nightfall from the valley of the Saco, and opened his heart to you in the evening, and passed through the Notch by sunrise, and was seen no more. Not a soul would ask, 'Who was he? Whither did the wanderer go?' But I cannot die till I have achieved my destiny. Then, let Death come! I shall have built my monument!"

Gallagher stopped for a moment and said aloud, "That's it. How could I be so dumb?"

Tobey, being the spokesperson for the little group reacts to Gallagher's sudden remark and says, "Gallagher...what's wrong? Are you going to finish the story?"

"Sorry kids. I just realized something."

Without further delay Gallagher finished reading the story to the children's delight.

***

14

~~~~~~

After the children left the bookshop, Gallagher immediately went to the Jackson police station to let Chief Perry know of his plans. Upon entering the station, Chief Perry directed him to his office while he was talking on the phone. He quickly hung up and showing an inquisitive look on his face says, "I just got off the phone with Lars from the Tavern. He has been trying to reach you. Anna told him you had just left the bookshop. I guess it's by Divine Providence you showed up here."

"That's an interesting declaration. What's going on?"

"I don't know what the significance of all of this is but Lars called and said the gorgeous woman who drives the Mercedes showed up at the Tavern about an hour ago. She was with a man he had never seen before. They sat at the far corner of the dining room and just ordered coffee. During the entire time they were there, it was obvious they were arguing about something. Her voice would get louder at times and he would grab onto her arm so she would quiet down. At one point Lars was about ready to go over and ask if there was problem and if she needed any help. She waved him off and said everything was fine. When they finally got up to leave she looked very distraught and hurried out of the Tavern."

"Is there anything else he might have heard during their conversation?"

"Just one thing... he heard the name Falkland two different times."

"Thanks Chief. I need to talk with Lars right away. I have a suspicion I know who the man was."

***

Gallagher walked over to the Village Tavern, entered the kitchen through the back door, and immediately pulled Lars aside, "Lars, can you describe the man who was with Jessica?"

"Who's Jessica?"

"The gorgeous woman you described who drives the Mercedes."

"Oh, that woman; I was about ready to punch the guy out but I'm glad she waved me off because he looked like someone you don't fool with. He was about six foot three and had a muscular and lean build. He had dark brown hair and brown eyes."

Gallagher nods and says, "That sounds like David Browning."

15

Gallagher left the Tavern, went directly to Eagle House, and then called Jonathan. "Valerie, is Jonathan there?"

"No...he said he received a call from his friend at the Observer. I guess he found something Jonathan was interested in; he should be there by now."

Gallagher wasted no time, arrived at the Jackson Observer's research building minutes later and entered the front lobby. A woman behind the reception desk exclaimed, "Gallagher Brady...good to see you. What brings you here today? Are you and Jonathan up to something?"

Gallagher smiles and says, "Good to see you too Judy. I guess you could say we are up to something but as you know its hush, hush for now."

"I totally understand. Jonathan is in the archive room down the hall."

"Thanks Judy."

Jonathan was busy writing down something when Gallagher walked in. Jonathan looked up and said, "I found a treasure while finding out about the treasure."

"You know something? I'm probably the only one who can figure out where you're coming from."

"Well...I'm a little excited about what I just found. We had some very old news clippings that were hidden in one of our vaults. One of them is a detailed account of a skirmish that took place in an archipelago back in 1809."

"You mean in the Falkland Islands?"

"That's the only thing that's missing, the actual name of the group of islands but it has to be the Falklands because listen to this."

Jonathan carefully opens up a folder, takes out a clipping, and begins reading; *"Twenty seamen were found dead scattered along several shorelines in an archipelago off the coast of South America. It is rumored a warship was seen leaving the islands shortly after they were found."*

"Who started the rumor?"

"It says further down in the article a lone survivor witnessed the massacre but died before he could say anymore."

Gallagher rubs his chin. "It's the third time the Falkland Islands comes into the picture. We read it in Chester Peabody's notebook and now this."

"It said their ship was found anchored about five hundred yards off shore riddled with cannon shot."

"I'm up on my history because it was my minor at Oxford but this is the first I've heard of this incident."

"There's a very good reason why you never learned about it at Oxford. The Jackson Observer's chief editor back in 1810 was a retired British sailor and his son was one of the seaman found slain."

"Wow! But that still doesn't explain why it was not recorded as a historical incident."

"No...but this does," Jonathan hands Gallagher a copy of an official document. It has the King of England's Coat of Arms as a letterhead.

Gallagher begins reading it aloud:

It is with deep regrets I send you this letter regarding the loss of your son at sea. I request that you, although grieving at this time, remain silent as to the details of this terrible tragedy. The welfare of England is involved and you, being a native son of the crown, hopefully will understand the delicate nature of this event and remain silent so the crown of England will continue to prosper.

Respectfully,

His Majesty, King George III

Gallagher handed back the document to Jonathan and said, "Well there's no doubt it's from the King of England."

Jonathan nods in agreement and says, "Why do you think it had to be kept secret?"

"It's my guess and I say it's just a guess. The King's own navy slaughtered those seamen. They were there probably seeking to find the treasure that was lost at sea in 1795. The unknown battleship seen leaving the area, most likely was a British warship. In order to avoid an international incident and avoid embarrassment, the personal request for restraint was required by the King."

"The ring Hawthorne's father found in the Falklands had to be part of that treasure," Jonathan reasoned.

"Well there are no details given about where exactly he found the ring in the notebook but the inscription on the ring leaves no doubt as to whom the rightful owner could have been. Hathorne and his crew may have been involved in recovering the treasure and then hid it somewhere in the Falklands; it's too early to tell."

"Why would he do such a risky thing?"

"Maybe he planned on returning one day to remove the treasure from wherever he hid it but he died before he was able to return. His son Nathaniel probably never realized the significance of the inscription on the ring."

"I find it hard to believe he wouldn't know its significance; he was an educated man. It could be the reason why he never spoke of it to anyone after it was stolen."

Gallagher thought for a moment. "You may be right. It is also possible he did speak of having the ring to John Browning in conversation. How else would John know of it and then eventually found an opportunity to steal it."

"We could go round and round with assumptions on what happened," Jonathan said.

"I know. We need proof."

"So what does that mean for our investigation?"

"This is where it gets interesting. I have a gut feeling David Browning is planning a trip to the Falklands and he wants to take Jessica with him. It could be why they were having that heated discussion in the Tavern."

"Heated is the right word for it judging by Lars reaction. What do you think he is expecting to find? The Falklands Islands cover an area of about 4,700 square miles. It would be like looking for a needle in a haystack."

"Maybe Nathaniel's father left behind some details on where he hid the treasure."

"Talk about a needle in a haystack. You are talking about a hundred and sixty-five years ago. Where do we start?"

"According to Peabody's notebook Nathaniel's father was a sea captain for the East India Marine Society. I am not sure if it still exists but we can find out. Hopefully we have some information at the Blackthorn Museum."

***

David Browning and Jessica Williams walked into the North Conway train station to purchase tickets to Boston via the Concord Station. David approached the clerk at the ticket booth. "I would like to purchase two tickets to Boston's South Station."

"I will be happy to do that for you," said Sandy. "The tickets will take you to Concord then you will connect on another train there, which will take you to South Station."

Jessica looked at David showing signs of anxiety over taking the trip. "I really would rather forget this whole thing. We both found out what we wanted about the ring and so let's get on with our lives."

"Do you realize what could be out there? With the information I have in this diary and other information I have been able to collect from other reliable sources, we are in a great position to find the rest of the treasure. The ring is just the tip of the iceberg."

Jessica shakes her head. "I'm sorry David but I really don't want to go with you. In all our conversations about the ring you never showed any signs of being interested in its monetary value, you were just like me, interested in our families history and love that was shared."

"Let's talk about this over dinner tonight. I'm positive I can convince you to join me." David urged.

Jessica nods her head but says nothing.

***

Gallagher and Jonathan left the museum with enough information to continue their investigation and made plans to go to the Peabody Essex Museum located in Salem, Massachusetts.

16

The following morning Gallagher and Jonathan started out for the Peabody Essex Museum. According to the information they had obtained, the trustees of the East India Marine Society transferred the East India Marine Society's records to the museum in 1910 after the Society suffered a financial collapse.

"It's very interesting how the Athenaeum Library and the Peabody Essex Museum have connections to Nathaniel Hawthorne's family." Jonathan said.

"Salem is definitely Hawthorne country. Even the House of Seven Gables is there, which was formally known as the Turner-Ingersoll Mansion."

"Do you really think we are going to find anything of any value at the museum?"

"If they have any records going back to the time when the Marine Society was established in 1799; there's a good possibility we will find something."

After a two and a half hour drive, they arrived at 161 Essex Street in Salem.

"What makes me wonder is, what could we possibly find that Chester Peabody hadn't already discovered?" Jonathan asked perplexed. "The Salem Athenaeum Library where you met Peabody is just up the street from here. He must have gleaned every morsel of information from this museum."

"It's possible but he may have missed something. Remember he did not have the information you were able to find from the Jackson Observer's archives about the twenty seaman found dead in the Falklands and in particular the document signed by King George. It appears he also didn't know about the inscription on the ring."

"That's true. This ought to be interesting."

They approached the reception desk. "Excuse me Miss but we were wondering if it's possible to examine the maritime records of Nathanael Hathorne, who was a sea captain for the East India Marine Society particularly during the years from 1799 to 1808."

"I think we can help you with that request," the receptionist replied. "You need to sign this register and state the reason for your interest."

Gallagher hesitated. "I was under the impression the records were available for public viewing."

"Yes they are but we like to keep track of what brings people to our museum."

"I understand," Gallagher replied. "I'm the proprietor of the Blackthorn Antiquarian Museum in Jackson, New Hampshire and I can see the value of keeping such a record. I'll have to incorporate that policy myself."

"I've heard of your museum. I would like to go there myself someday."

Gallagher wrote down the reason for their visit and then she escorted them to an elevator. "We keep all the records downstairs and they are arranged by their dates. You should have no trouble finding them."

"Thank you Miss."

They walked into a large room filled with numerous file cabinets. They quickly found the cabinet marked 1795 -1810.

"What are we looking for exactly," Jonathan asked.

"We know that Hathorne dropped anchor in the Falklands in 1799 according to Peabody's notebook. He found the ring while he was exploring the islands because of having certain knowledge he gained from the natives that a British ship had sank off the coast in 1795. What the notebook does not mention is the link to King George. What we need to know is if Hathorne ever returned to the Falklands."

After a few hours of searching through all the records pertaining to Hathorne's travels, they found one interesting notation.

"Look at this," Gallagher said excitedly. "After coming back to the States in 1801 he returned to his home on 27 Union Street."

Jonathan pulled out the map listing the directions to the museum. "According to this map his birthplace was moved to 27 Hardy Street in 1958, which is about seven blocks away from here."

"If my memory serves me correctly, Nathaniel Hawthorne was born in 1804."

"Yes and we know that his father died in Suriname in 1808," Jonathan added.

"Okay that should narrow things down. We need to see if Hathorne left any information on what he did from 1804 thru 1807."

After another hour of digging through several notes and nautical charts, Gallagher said triumphantly, "I found Hathorne's personal calendar. He did some traveling through our area in the White Mountains while on vacation. He lists a number of Inns he and his wife Betsey stayed at while in the area but there are no specific dates."

"The only one that's mentioned by name is 'Under the Elm Inn.'"

Jonathan nods and says, "I know of the place. It's in Northwood, New Hampshire."

"Is it still there?"

"The building is but it has been unoccupied for as long as I can remember. I drove by it some years ago while investigating a story and thinking what a strange name for an Inn. What else does his calendar say?"

"He had circled the date December 28th 1807 and next to it the words Falkland Islands. It appears, according to most of these reports, the East India Marine Society made several trips down to Tierra del Fuego and then to Cape Horn before returning to Portsmouth, New Hampshire."

"It looks like he was planning to visit the Falklands Islands again while he was down there; possibly to look for more of King George's treasure," Jonathan reasoned.

"If he did make that trip, there are no records of his return. It looks like Suriname was as far as he got on his return trip."

Gallagher returned all the records and charts back into the filing cabinet marked 1804 thru 1806. He then went to the cabinet marked 1808 thru 1810.

"What are you looking for now?" Jonathan asked.

"There must be something about Hathorne's death. Also, what happened to his crew?"

"What are you getting at?"

"Remember what you found in the Observer's archives about the twenty seamen who were found dead along the shores of the Falklands?"

"How could I forget?"

"It mentioned one survivor who witnessed the massacre but died before he could tell anything more about it. I have a suspicion that one survivor was Hathorne himself. He may have been able to sail back to Suriname by himself, which may account for his weakened condition and subsequently he came down with Yellow Fever."

Gallagher began looking through the reports and came upon one dated December 28, 1807.

"It says here he sailed on this last voyage on December 28, 1807, on the Nabby bound for Suriname, or Dutch Guiana. Less than a month later, on January 9, 1808, his wife gave birth to Maria Louisa. A few months later, in early April of 1808, she received the news of her husband's death from yellow fever in Suriname."

"That doesn't go along with your thinking. It doesn't mention anything about the Falklands at all."

"That doesn't mean he didn't go there. I think he went to the Falklands off the record and then returned to Suriname where he died."

"Too much speculation; we need more evidence," Jonathan stressed.

"I was hoping to avoid this but one of us needs to go to Suriname and find out if he left any clue to what really happened."

Jonathan hesitates for a moment. "The letter from King George seems to indicate the seamen were British subjects. Why do you think Hawthorne's crew was involved?"

"The only thing I can think of is Hawthorne's last trip to the Falklands was off the radar. He may have hired a British crew with the lure of offering them some of the treasure."

***

Later that day Gallagher and Jonathan talked over their plans. Gallagher is to fly out of Boston the next morning for Suriname, which is on the northeastern coast of South America and land at Johan Adolf Pengal International Airport. From there he will go to the American Embassy and seek out any information he can on where Nathaniel's father spent his last days before he died. Jonathan was to travel to Raymond on the shores of Lake Sebago to find out more about the mysterious David Browning.

17

The next day Gallagher's plane touched down smoothly in Suriname. It was late afternoon and he did not have much time before darkness was to set in. He called a cab and was taken to the American Embassy. He gets the information he needs and is taken to a small hotel to register and drop off his luggage. The cab driver waited patiently outside the hotel while Gallagher changed his clothes and collected the necessary gear.

The landscape was changing quickly as they traveled deeper into to a more primitive jungle-like environment. After driving for more than hour, Gallagher arrived at the hospital located in a remote village outside of the capitol city of Paramaribo. He told the cabby he would more than compensate him for his time if he waited for a couple of hours while he took care of business inside. The cabby reluctantly agreed.

Gallagher walked towards the entrance of the hospital expecting to find extremely poor conditions inside but to his surprise, he saw a newly remodeled state of the art medical facility.

A man seeing him entering the lobby approaches him and says, "Welcome to our humble hospital. My name is Dr. William Benjamin. Can I be of some assistance? Are you here to see one of our patients?"

Gallagher shakes his head and says, "I believe the patient I'm inquiring about has long since died?"

"I'm sorry, I don't understand."

Gallagher smiles and says, "I hardly do myself. Let me get to the point. Back in the year 1808 a man by the name of Nathaniel Hathorne, who was the father of the famous writer, Nathaniel Hawthorne supposedly died in this hospital. I don't know if you have records going back that far but the spelling of his last name is spelled without a W."

"I'm sorry Mr...?"

My name is Gallagher Brady. I am a friend of the family from Jackson, New Hampshire. I've traveled many miles to find out anything I can about the deceased."

"Jackson, New Hampshire; I know it well. I did my postgraduate studies at the UNH before going on to medical school in New York. I have been here for a little over a year and I know the medical records that existed back then had been destroyed when a tribal war ravaged the hospital in 1865. The ruins of the original west wing of the hospital still remain but I don't know what you could find there; it's just a pile of rubble. Everyone is encouraged not to go there."

Gallagher walks over to a window and sees the ruins. "How come it was never cleaned up after all these years?"

"Some of the natives have this superstition about disturbing the site where many of their family members were killed during the tribal war that destroyed a big section of the hospital and most of the village."

"Is there any problem with me taking a look?"

"What do you expect to find?"

"I'll know it when I see it."

"Be my guest. If all of sudden you get some company, do not react as though you're afraid. If you remain calm and go about your business, they will leave you alone. Sometimes, they think visitors are called by their dead relatives to visit them; like a said, superstition."

Gallagher left the hospital and began walking towards the ruins. The sun was setting and he realized he better work quickly before complete darkness made it impossible to see anything in the thick jungle. He looked back for a moment and noticed the cabby had left the area. Temporarily unfazed by the cabby's departure he continued on to find anything he could to bring back with him so as not to make the whole trip a big waste of time.

The walls of the old west wing of the hospital were barely standing because of absence of a roof. Through the years, heavy tropical rains had washed much of the mud and mortar away from the stones weakening the walls to the point of them leaning towards collapse. Gallagher was beginning to think it was an impossible task to find anything significant. He then wandered into an area and saw the walls partially covered by what was left of the roof. He looked around and figured he was standing in what was once a patient's room. The walls were still solid as he felt his way through the dark room. He took out his flashlight and aimed it around the room and then something caught his eye. Just as he was about to stoop down to take a better look a voice spoke out of the darkness in what sounded English with a Dutch accent. "You shouldn't be here. The natives don't like trespassers."

Gallagher startled by the voice, turns around. "Who are you?"

"Unofficially I'm what you call the law around here. I look out for the interests of the natives."

"I was told I could examine these ruins by Dr. Benjamin. He said the natives might not bother me if they think I'm visiting their dead relatives."

"Is that what you are doing here?"

"Not quite. You wouldn't believe me if I told you."

"Try me; I'm real curious because you are the fourth person to come snooping around here in about a week. There have been others in the past."

"Really...! Do you mind telling me who they were?" Gallagher asked.

"They don't volunteer their names but they smell like MI6. Do you mind telling me who you are?"

Gallagher ignored his question. "I take it you don't care for the British Secret Service."

"Not particularly."

"Can I ask your reason?"

"Britain has been trying to get this country back ever since they lost it back 1667. There has been a lot of blood spilled over this piece of land."

"It's kind of a longtime to hold a grudge; don't you think?"

"Tell that to my dead brother; he was killed by an MI6 agent by mistake two years ago. They go poking their nose where it doesn't belong because they revel in the fact that at one time the sun never set on British soil. I believe Britain and the United States are the world's bullies. Just because a particular nation does not quite agree with their form of politics, they use force to persuade. History has proven it to be so."

"I guess you have more than a grudge. Well I don't talk politics except with a good friend of mine back home."

"Where's back home?"

"The White Mountains of New Hampshire in the good old USA. You know, one of the bullies."

"Well don't mind me. I could tell you were not MI6. Go about your business. The natives are quiet today."

"To answer your earlier question, my name is Gallagher Brady and I'm a book collector and was hoping to find some information about the father of a famous author by the name of Nathaniel Hathorne."

The man's eyes opened wide. "Don't know the name."

"It's understandable. He was a patient in this hospital back in 1808. I believe this is where he actually died. Did any of the others enter this section of the hospital?"

"Yes they did. Interestingly they were looking around just about where you're standing."

"Did they find anything?"

"If they did they didn't volunteer that either. Some of my friends gave one of them a real scare and he left suddenly."

"Sounds strange for a MI6 agent; they don't scare easily."

"Who else would be interested in this place?"

"Maybe the Queen of England...."

"Why would the Royal Crown be interested in this hole in the wall?"

"It all goes back to 1795. I would like to give you a history lesson but I need to get back home."

"Well... I hope you find what you're looking for? I will let you be. Good day."

Once the man left the area, Gallagher approached the back wall of the room and shined his light upon a partially crumbled foundation stone that had scratch marks on it. As he got closer, he realized it was a small X. He took out his Swiss Army knife and carefully dug around the stone to remove the already loosened mud and mortar. After several minutes, the stone came loose and he was able to remove it. He shined his light into the empty space

103

and saw a rolled up letter. He pulled it out and began reading it to himself:

On 10th day of June in the year 1799, my hired crew and I dropped anchor off the shores of East Falkland Island to replenish supplies at Port Stanley. We spent several days exploring many of the inlets on the island. While exploring one of them I came across several gold coins that had washed ashore. My interest grew because of recent information I had gained from a native I met named Louis about a Spanish ship sinking off the coast of this archipelago some four years earlier. The ship had recently been in a battle with a British warship, which was secretly transporting the King of England's personal treasure to the islands because of the ongoing war with France. Upon destroying the British ship and killing the entire crew, the Spanish ship was later torn apart by an ocean storm as it rounded Cape Horn. The badly damaged ship was able to float for more than four hundred nautical miles because of strong trade winds and finally sank off the coast of the archipelago. Its crew and cargo were all lost at sea and King George's treasure was scattered to the oceans floor. Louis told me these details including all the blood that spilled because of the lost treasure. I asked Louis what happened to the treasure and he said the natives of the island sent experienced deep-water divers to gather up what they could of the treasure and bury it so no one would be able to find it. I asked him why they would do such a thing and he simply said their treasure was their paradise home and they had no need for gold and silver.

After I found the coins, my crew and I continued to search the inlet and we came across a strongbox partially uncovered by the oceans constant thrashing of the shoreline during a recent storm. When we opened the box, I found a gold ring, a helmet, and a letter sealed inside a glass wine bottle. As I was about ready to break the bottle so I could read the letter I saw several uniformed men marching in our direction. We quickly buried the strongbox where we found it then we left the inlet, before they reached us. We returned to our dinghy before the soldiers arrived and rowed to our ship. Fearing to return to the inlet, we decided to set sail and return home to Portsmouth, New Hampshire.

I eventually settled down in Salem, Massachusetts where my son Nathaniel was born. During my time in Salem, I wrote my last will and testament and left my son the gold ring I had found, which is one of three things I had taken back with me. My health had been failing me for some time and I wanted him to have the ring so upon his betrothal to his future wife he would have a priceless treasure that was once undoubtedly on the finger of a Queen. I have never divulged the origin of the ring to anyone, including my wife Elizabeth, because of my concern for her safety. The executor of my estate, Mr. Robert Manning will handle all my affairs upon my death. I planned to return to recover the strongbox we had buried on our next trip to South America.

On September 28, 1807, I rejoined my crew and we set sail for Surihame. After picking up our cargo, we planned to continue south and drop anchor on shores of East Falkland Island where we buried the strongbox. Our journey was without incident and we successfully arrived in Suriname. We picked up some rare Asian artwork and replenished our fresh water and food supply before continuing our trip. We spent only two days here when I began developing symptoms of Yellow Fever. I told my crew to leave without me and search for the strongbox to recover what we left behind. I said I would join them on the next available packet to the Falklands after my fever broke but in my heart, I knew I would never see them again.

My days in this hospital have turned into weeks and my condition has worsened. Word was sent to me that my crew was attacked and all were killed but one by an unknown group. I fear my death is imminent and I grieve for my crew. The fever will not yield and my thinking ability has become cloudy. To the finder of this letter, I have described in as much detail as I could on my travels since I discovered the treasure of King George of England.

NH

Gallagher concealed the letter, and left the ruins of the hospitals ruined west wing and returned to the lobby of the hospital. He called for another cab and left for his hotel room, satisfied he had found Hathorne's deathbed and had gained more insight on the last days of his life; in particular the origin of the gold ring.

Upon returning to his hotel room, he noticed two men waiting in the lobby. One of them approached

Gallagher and said, "Excuse me but can I ask where you have been during the past three hours?"

"Who's asking?"

One of the men shows Gallagher his badge. "Special Police? What's going on?" Gallagher asked.

"Did you take a cab from this hotel?"

"Yes I did. Gallagher looked at his watch. "About three hours ago. Why?"

"A cab driver was found after he had been severely beaten about a mile from here. We were wondering if you knew anything about it."

"If it's the same cabby, I asked him to wait for me while I visited the hospital. He said he would but I noticed he drove off not long after I went inside the hospital. Is he going to be alright?"

"It is too early to tell. Would you mind coming with us? The cab driver is being cared for at our police station; a doctor is with him right now. We thought he would not make the ride to the hospital with the amount of blood he has already lost. He has also refused to talk with us for some reason."

"Just let me go to my room for a minute to drop off a couple things. I will be right back."

Twenty minutes later Gallagher enters the police station and sees the cabby lying on cot. Gallagher looks at the doctor working on him. "Is it okay to talk with him?"

"He's barely awake. We had to give him some morphine for the pain."

Gallagher went over to him. "Excuse me but do you remember me?"

The cabby barely nods his head.

"Can you tell us what happened?"

The cabby looked up at Gallagher and handed him a note, then expired.

Gallagher looked at the note. *"They will not give up!"*

Gallagher looks at the police officer standing next to him. "Do you know what he meant by this?"

"No...but let me ask you this. Why were you at the hospital? Were you visiting a patient there?"

"He was a patient about one hundred and sixty years ago."

"What? Are you some kind of wise guy?"

Gallagher pulls out his badge. "I'm here on an investigation and for security reasons I will not say anymore. There are too many eyes and ears around here and I believe my cabby paid the price. If you have no other questions I must get back to my hotel room."

"We have no reason to keep you. You may go."

"That's it? No argument?"

"What you have just told us is consistent with what has been going on around here lately."

"You mean before I arrived here?"

"Yes and that's all I will tell you."

Without any further questions, Gallagher returned to his hotel room. When he entered to his room, he found it had been ransacked. He immediately went to the widow and pulled down the shade and Hathorne's letter fell out. He rolled it back up, packed his things and left for the airport.

***

18

In harmony with the plans they made the day before, Jonathan traveled to the town of Raymond to the shores of Lake Sebago. David Browning's home was listed at 2 Indian Point Road. The road turned to sand the closer it got to the shoreline of the lake. He quickly spotted a modern looking deckhouse and approached the back entrance. The name on the mailbox read Browning. He noticed several days' worth of newspapers sitting on his doorstep. Jonathan rang the bell several times but no one came to the door. He was ready to knock when a man approached him from behind. "Mr.... we haven't seen or heard from David for about four days now. My wife and I were about ready to call the police and then we saw you pull up. Are you the police or some kind of detective?"

"I'm a reporter for the Jackson Observer. You say you haven't seen David for four days?"

"As you can see we are sort of close to each other around here so nothing gets by us without us noticing. We look out for each other. What made us suspicious was because his car has never moved from the driveway for the four days he has been missing. We have a policy to let each other know if we were going away for an extended period. He left no word."

Jonathan hesitated for a moment. "You wouldn't happen to have a shot gun on you?"

"No sir! Why would you think that?"

Jonathan laughed. "Experience I guess. Did you notice anything else out of the ordinary?"

"About four or five days ago David had a visitor. We had come home from shopping and we noticed a fancy red car parked behind David's."

"How long was it here?"

"I would say about two hours. I don't know how long he was here before we came home?"

"Thank you. You have been very helpful. I'm going let myself in and see what I can find out."

The neighbors left Jonathan confident he was not a thief. Jonathan forced the door open and immediately smelled the strong sent of urine as he entered the house. He walked into the bedroom where he found a man gagged and tied to a bed. He immediately pulled the gag off and saw the man was still breathing but barely conscious. He got a glass of cold water and splashed some on the man's face and he finally came to. Besides urine, there was a strong scent of whiskey in the room. The man opened his eyes and looked around the room then looked at Jonathan. "Who are you?"

"My name is Jonathan Henry and I'm a reporter for the Jackson Observer. My associate, Gallagher Brady and I are involved in an investigation having to do with a gold ring found on Mount Willey. In the process of our investigation your name came to our attention; that is if you are David Browning."

"I am and thank God you showed up! I thought I was going to die here. How long have I been tied to this bed?"

"According to your nice neighbor's about four days. It appears you have been duped by an agent of the British government."

"It doesn't surprise me now that I think about it. He came to my house claiming to be from my insurance company wanting to do an assessment on my property, promising me he could save me quite a bit of money by changing the type of home owners policy I had. The next thing I knew, I am strapped to this bed and he is forcing whiskey down my throat. The man demanded me to tell him where I kept my uncle's personal diary, which surprised me he even knew about it. I refused to tell him because there was obviously private information recorded in it that I never wanted revealed. He kept pouring the whiskey down my throat between his demands. I thought I was going to drown before I got drunk. I think I passed out before I could tell him anything but I'm not sure. It feels like the whiskey found its way out. My pants are soaked."

"Well I don't know if you told him anything but he found the diary and we think he's planning to fly to the Falkland Islands."

"I kept the diary in my nightstand."

Jonathan opened the draw to the nightstand. "The diary is missing but he left a note."

David read the note to himself. "I need to call someone right away; she may be in danger."

"It wouldn't be Jessica Williams; would it?"

"How in the world would you know that? First of all Jessica and I have never met; we have just talked on the phone."

Jonathan grimaced. "I was afraid of that because she met a man, who I now believe is a MI6 agent, who posed as your insurance agent. Jessica had no reason to think it was not you. He also may have convinced her to travel to the Falklands with him. I think he is using her as a cover. You know the happy couple on vacation able to blend right into the landscape."

"They have to be stopped."

"What does the note say?"

"It says Jessica will be harmed if he's followed."

"We have him on our radar. We know what his plans are. I will fill you in on our plans after you get yourself cleaned up and you have something to eat. Do you think you need any medical attention?"

"No, I'm alright. I'll be good as new after I shower and have something in my stomach. Wow! I can't believe I was so fooled."

"Don't blame yourself. My associate was also fooled by him and that's hard to do."

***

After a long hot shower and some sandwiches at the local deli, David and Jonathan left Lake Sebago and headed for Jackson. David accepted the offer to stay at Eagle House temporarily while the police dusted his home for fingerprints. Even though he had never met Jessica, David had grown attached to her because of the several phone conversations they had through the years over the unfortunate tragedy of their distant relations. Jessica called David one day with the hopes of him being a distant relation to John Browning. When she found out he was, they kept in touch my letter and by phone, even though they lived many miles away from each other. Both knew they needed to meet right away when they heard about the gold ring being found on Mount Willey. David had written down the place, the day and the time he was to meet with her on his wall calendar. It was with that bit of helpful information the agent was able to meet Jessica at the appointed place and time and no questions would be asked. After arriving at Eagle House, Jonathan arranged to show David the ring the next morning.

***

Gallagher's plane touched down in Concord and he met Anna who had been anxiously waiting for him at the train station. From there they traveled to North Conway and arrived at the train station one hour later. From there they drove to Eagle House.

Gallagher swiped his keycard to open the electric gate and drove up the long winding driveway. "Are we happy to see you," Jonathan exclaimed as he met him at the front door.

Gallagher smiled showing he was glad to be home. "That goes for me too. I was so happy to get out of Suriname. I thought I was going to be there forever. It's not a friendly place."

Gallagher walked into the living room where Helen and Bill were anxiously waiting to hear what happened in Suriname.

"Did you find anything?" Helen blurted out.

"I did. I saw the hospital and the room where Hathorne spent his last days, which was amazing considering its condition. I found some scratch marks on a foundation stone in the shape of an X on the back wall of the room. I scraped away the mud and crusty mortar around the stone and carefully removed it from the wall. Inside was a deep indentation, most likely dug by Hathorne and I found this...."

Gallagher hands Jonathan the rolled up letter written on brown stationary. Jonathan unrolls it and lays it on the table. After reading it aloud so everyone could hear he said, "What a very sad but amazing story."

"It's a sad story but one that has taken on a new dimension. According to a mysterious Dutchman I talked with in Suriname, at least four people have already been there snooping around; as recent as a few days before I showed up. According to the Dutchman, they entered Hathorne's room but apparently didn't notice the X etched on the stone."

Jonathan shakes his head. "A lot of good it does having it other than we know where the ring came from. As far as the strongbox is concerned; that's probably already been found."

"I doubt it because why would there be so much interest in where Hathorne died. What he found in the Falklands is not as much of a secret as he thought."

"Good point."

Gallagher gave Jonathan a curious look "What have you been doing while I've been gone? Anna said I should hear all the details from you."

"I went to David Browning's home like we talked about. I found him tied up and gagged in his bedroom. He had been like that for at least four days. He was dehydrated and very hungry. The man claiming to be David might be a British agent. He had taken John Browning's diary from David's nightstand. That's why he knew so much when he talked with you at the museum."

"I had a feeling he was MI6," Gallagher said shaking his head in disgust."

Jonathan studied the letter more closely and held it up to the light. "Did you notice the watermark?"

Gallagher looked surprised at the question. "I didn't notice it, but I must admit, it was very dark where I read it."

"Look at the middle of the page. Can you make out what it says?"

Gallagher picked up the letter, brought it closer to the light, and saw what Jonathan was referring too.

Turner-Ingersoll Mansion

"It's a watermark alright. It says; Turner-Ingersoll Mansion; this proves Hathorne was there and was able to get a hold of their stationary."

Jonathan nods. "Yeah...I think we need to make another trip to Salem."

"Are you thinking what I'm thinking?"

"He may have left a clue in the Turner-Ingersoll Mansion."

"Precisely...! It is the reason he wrote the letter on their stationary. He knew his health was failing before his trip to Suriname and wanted to leave a clue in case he never returned. This really emphasizes how important he thought the letter was that he found in the strongbox. In his letter, he said the ring was *one* of three things he brought back with him. I think he also brought back the letter and the helmet."

Gallagher goes into his library and comes back with a large one volume encyclopedia. "According to this, the mansion was built 1668 for Captain John Turner, and it stayed with the family for three generations. The mansion became famous by American author Nathaniel Hawthorne's 1851 novel *The House of the Seven Gables*. The house and its surrounding area are a National Historic Landmark District. It also says something very interesting. The very house Hawthorne was born in was originally on Union Street then was moved in 1958 and is now on Hardy Street, immediately adjacent to the Turner-Ingersoll Mansion on Derby Street, which is now called the House of Seven Gables."

"Do you think Nathaniel Hawthorne, the author, may have gotten his idea to write about the House of Seven Gables from his father, Nathaniel Hathorne, the sea captain?"

"I don't know but this goes on to say, 'Hawthorne's grandfather purchased the house on Union Street in 1772. Nathaniel was born in that house on July 4, 1804, and lived there until the age of four. Most of the interior has been preserved intact.'"

"I'm now getting confused," Jonathan admits.

"When I put all the information we have gathered so far we get this; Nathaniel's father found the treasure in 1799. He returned to the States and did some traveling and in 1804, his son Nathaniel was born. While living on Union Street, which was about five blocks away from where the Turner-Ingersoll Mansion is located, Hathorne may have frequented the mansion and may have had opportunity to hide what he found in the Falklands somewhere inside the mansion."

"That's a lot of speculation! Why do you think he would hide it in the mansion and not his own home?"

"Forethought..."

"What do you mean?"

"Hawthorne's own house has been moved right across the street from the Turner-Ingersoll Mansion for obvious commercial purposes because Nathaniel made the mansion famous by writing about it in his story, the House of Seven Gables. It is unlikely his father would have hidden something of value in his own home. He would've known the Turner-Ingersoll Mansion was the best place to hide something of importance because it was already a historic landmark and would not be moved or destroyed, where as his own home could have eventually been moved or destroyed by eminent domain."

Jonathan thinks for a moment. "When you think about it, the House of Seven Gables was written way after Nathaniel's father died. He did not even know his son would become a famous author. Because of that he would've had no idea his own home would someday become a historical landmark itself."

"That's right. It would make perfect sense to hide something important like a letter in a building which already had historical significance."

Helen interrupts their conversation. "I'm sure you might find this interesting as you gather all your evidence. I received a surprise call from old friend of mine from my Oxford days; a Professor Dean Cook. He was a Professor of British history and a leading authority on the Royal Monarchy of England. He's retired now and we had lost touch with each for several years. I think at one time he had feelings for me but I thought he was a little too eccentric my taste. Anyways in talking with Dean, I mentioned about your investigation and in particular finding a ring with the Coat of Arms of the King of England inscribed on it."

"What was his reaction?"

"He seemed to hesitate at first then he told me the Royal family has a secret force of highly trained agents called the Royal Guardians. They are similar to the Pontifical Swiss Guard of the Holy See stationed at the Vatican in Rome. They have been in existence for centuries with the sole purpose of protecting the interests of the Royal family separate from the British government. Many times, they have been at cross-purposes with each other. You may want to talk with him yourself because he was deeply interested in what you found; now even more so after finding Hathorne's letter. In his letter, he mentioned the finger of a Queen. That will definitely spark Dean's interest."

Gallagher noticed a troubled look on Helen's face. "Is something bothering you?"

"As I think about it he hesitated but did not sound surprised."

"Well if we are dealing with the group he mentioned called the Royal Guardians this whole thing is getting very interesting because at the same time we could be dealing with MI6 agents; which to me proves we are talking about more than just gold and silver. It definitely has something to do with the contents of the letter. I think

119

whoever these guys are; they are connecting the ring with the letter."

"What are you getting at?" Helen asked.

"It's seems unlikely a treasure going back centuries would have the interest of the British government and the Royal family. The letter was important enough for Hathorne to take it with him and then hide it somewhere. The Royal Guardians may be the ones lurking about in our backyard right now because they somehow know of the gold rings connection to British Royalty. How they know of that fact, is beyond me but I am sure an organization like that has its resources. As you said, after reading Hathorne's letter he mentioned the ring was on the finger of a Queen and with the knowledge we have of what the inscription on the ring means, is now making more sense."

"While you're figuring that out I think you should talk with the real David Browning whose upstairs recuperating from his ordeal."

"That's right," Anna said. "What about Jessica and David? If you are planning another treasure hunt in Salem you won't be able to get back in time to stop them from leaving."

"Leaving where?"

"I called the train station while you were in Suriname and talked with Sandy. Going on what details you described to me, I gave Sandy the description of Jessica and the imposter posing as David. She said a couple had been in the other day and purchased two tickets to Concord Station along with a connecting ticket to Boston's South Station. I thought of your concern about David planning to travel to the Falklands so I called Logan Airport and there are flights regularly going to Argentina."

"Did she say when they were going?"

"Tomorrow at noon..."

"It doesn't give us much time. I shouldn't go because they both know who I am and I need to have Jonathan with me in Salem. This is where a woman's touch can come in. Aunt Helen, how would you like to get in on some action?"

"What kind of action?"

"Right now Jessica needs a mother type to convince her not to go with the man who she believes to be David Browning. I need you and the real David to show up at the train station and interfere with her plans to leave on the noon train tomorrow with that imposter. I will let Chief Perry know of our plans and he will have one of his officer's close by in case there's any trouble."

"Are you expecting trouble?"

"I have a feeling Jessica is being forced to go through with it and she might cause a scene if she tries to back out of it."

"What exactly do you want me to do?"

"You have always been able to think your way through things; Jonas taught you well. I know you will do the right thing."

***

19

The next morning Gallagher and Jonathan left for Salem to visit the Turner-Ingersoll Mansion now called the House of Seven Gables Museum, while Helen and David Browning were planning their surprise visit to the North Conway train station.

Since making their plans, Gallagher absorbed himself in as much research as he could on finding out about Nathaniel Hawthorne's family and the families of Jessica Williams and David Browning. What it was looking like to him was a belated love story in the making. Two individuals bound together by a common desire to find a wedding ring that would have made them cousins by the marriage if Jessica's great grandmother and David's great uncle had met each other on that infamous night. Instead, the common interest they have shared together was leading to something unexpected and very special.

***

Helen and David walked into the train station at eleven thirty, allowing enough time to intercept the couple.

"How are you today Helen?" asked Sandy at the ticket booth. "It's so good to see you."

"I'm well Sandy. I would like you to meet by my good friend David who is visiting from Cheshire England. We knew each other when we attended school together at Oxford. I thought I would show him the sights in Boston."

"It's nice to meet you David. I know Helen will be able to show you a good time in that cultural Mecca. Is your husband Bill joining you?"

"He plans on meeting us there later today. First, he had some business to attend to in Worcester. He left early this morning."

Sandy hands Helen the tickets and then they walk over and take a seat in the lobby waiting for the action to begin.

David starts rubbing his chin. "This beard you made out of an old wig of yours is driving me crazy."

"I'm sorry about that," Helen whispered. "It was meant to be worn on top of the head, not hanging from someone's chin."

"I hope the agent who visited my home doesn't recognize me in this thing."

Helen looks David over and says, "I really know who you are and you are really fooling me right now."

They both start laughing and then Helen sees Sandy's signal. "David, they are coming," Helen whispered.

Helen sees Jessica first and notices she had been crying. The imposter is right behind her, grabs her arm, and leads her to the boarding area. They all waited for several minutes then Helen looks at her watch and sees its ten minutes past twelve. She whispers in David's ear. "The train is running late. My husband must have accomplished his mission."

Helen gets up, walks over to Jessica, and says, "Excuse me but you look very familiar. I have a cousin named Elizabeth who used to live in Moultonborough, not far from here. You look just like her."

Jessica, with a look of surprise says, "I'm from Moultonborough. My name is Jessica Williams. It is a very small village on the lake and I don't know anyone by that name; especially anyone who looks like me. What's her last name?"

"Adams."

Now a more startled look appears on Jessica's face but she remains silent so as not to draw the attention of the imposter.

Helen then asks, "Are you traveling for business or pleasure?"

The imposter starts to squirm and impatiently asks, "Excuse me lady. We are waiting for a train and it's apparently running late. Are you waiting for the same train?"

"Yes we are. It should be here any minute. I cannot imagine what's keeping it. It was nice to meet you Jessica. I hope you both have a nice trip."

Helen reaches to shake her hand and gives her a tiny note. Helen looks into her eyes and says in a whisper, "Read it now!"

The imposter is busy looking further down the tracks hoping to catch sight of the train when it finally rounds the bend. This allows Jessica the time she needs to read the note discreetly. Her eyes widen as she reads it...*'The man you're with is not*

David Browning but the man with me in a disguise is; don't get on the train!'

A look of panic comes over Jessica's face. While the imposter is not looking, Helen grabs Jessica by the arm, hurries her into Sandy's office, and locks the door. The imposter turns around to look for Jessica as the train starts slowing down. He notices she is gone and a look of rage appears on his face. Realizing he has was fooled, decides not to make a scene, he reluctantly boards the train in a panic. At the same time another man who had been sitting by himself in a corner jumps up and leaps onto the train at the last minute. Once the train was safely out of sight David Browning quickly removed his disguise. Jessica looked at him. "David?"

"Yes Jessica, it's your pen pal."

She immediately runs into his arms." I have been so confused. That person, whoever he was, was so different from the David I have come to know in all the years we have corresponded with each other. I should have guessed because I said certain things and it was as though he did not know what I was saying. It all makes sense now."

David holds her gently. "We should have met years ago when we found out about our common interest in finding the ring. I feel as though we have missed a lot of moments we could have shared together."

Helen, overhearing the conversation says, "The way you two sound, you might be think it's too late for a relationship. Let me tell you something. I have waited almost all my life to find the right man for me and it was worth the wait. The two of you have many years ahead of you. Let this be the start of something greater than what you've already experienced together."

Jessica smiles, showing her genuine happiness and says, "This is too good to be true. I am beginning to think the wedding ring is so insignificant now that we have finally met each other. I don't care about the ring anymore."

David nods. "I think our pursuit of the ring was just a way of fulfilling what never took place between my great uncle and your great grandmother."

"I believe so too."

Helen looks at her watch and says, "Why don't we go back to my home at Eagle House and enjoy some food and champagne to celebrate this wonderful union you both have just experienced. My husband Bill should be back from Concord by now. I'm curious to hear how he was able to delay the train."

Before they all leave Helen goes over to Sandy. "Do you know who that man was who jumped on the train in the last second?"

"All I know is when he purchased his ticket he spoke with a very elegant English accent. Maybe he was a secret agent or something."

Helen laughs. "You may not be too far off on that one."

Sandy laughs herself and says, "I probably have just seen too many James Bond movies lately."

***

Gallagher and Jonathan arrived at the Turner-Ingersoll Mansion about two in the afternoon. The mansion, now a museum, was open for visitors. The building has three floors and a cellar. They both realized the standard tour of the house would not include the cellar but in their minds if anything Nathaniel's father was to hide, it would have probably been in the cellar. The trick was to find a way to get into the cellar without drawing attention.

As they toured the many rooms, they looked for a door leading to the cellar. After the thirty-minute tour ended, they observed no door leading to the cellar. Gallagher whispers to Jonathan, "Did you see the impressive bookcase in the library we passed through?"

"Yeah,... what about it?"

"I'm going to ask the tour guide if we can take a closer look at the books. Maybe we'll be able to find something there."

"Like what?"

"I thought the cellar would be the most obvious place to look but since we can't find a door the next best place to look is in the library."

"It makes sense coming from a book collector," Jonathan replied.

Gallagher walked over to the reception area, sees the young woman who had just given them the tour of the house. "Excuse me Miss, my name is Gallagher Brady and I'm here with my associate

Jonathan Henry to gather some information on a book he's writing. Maybe you've heard of his first book, 'The Mysterious Mansions of Newport'."

"Actually I've read the book. I have been working here for about five years now and many visitors have commented on the mansions in Newport and comparing them to this one in age and architecture. Out of curiosity, I picked up Mr. Henry's book a few years ago and read it cover to cover. I really found it interesting. I wish I had it with me so he could sign it."

"I think Jonathan would be happy to come by sometime in the future to sign it for you. You would be doing him a big favor if you allowed him to browse through some of the books you have here for his latest book."

"Please go right ahead. Our next tour will be in two hours so you will have plenty of time. Some of those books belonged to the original owner of the mansion."

Gallagher thanked her and walked back to where Jonathan was waiting and they both entered the museum's library. Several works of fiction lined the shelves by such authors as Poe, Melville, Stevenson, Emerson and Thoreau. Many were original editions bound in leather. In Gallagher's mind, he was looking for one book in particular, the Holy Bible. It has been his experience in the past if a person wanted to keep something of importance in a safe place, the Bible was the ideal choice. After several minutes of combing through the many shelves, Gallagher spotted a family size King James

Bible. By the condition of the leather, it looked very old and well used. He took the Bible off the shelf and carefully placed it on a table and began looking through it to see if something stood out. Jonathan sees what he's looking at and says, "If that Bible is as old as it looks, I'd be very surprised if Hathorne hid anything inside and it would still be there after all these years."

"I don't think he would've hidden the actual letter in here. It would have easily been found by someone after all these years. But there might be a clue in here as to where he did hide it."

After several minutes went by Jonathan said, "You're looking through those pages like you are looking for the actual treasure of King George."

Gallagher looked up at Jonathan with a big smile. "You're a genius. Why didn't I think of that?"

"Wait a minute; think of what?"

"Treasure....The Bible refers to God's Word as being a treasure in several places."

Gallagher flips back to the inside cover. "This was the family Bible of Captain John Turner, the original owner of this house. It had to have been here when Nathaniel's father was living just a few blocks down the road."

Jonathan sat down beside Gallagher and took a closer look. "Do you have any idea where to look?"

"The only verse that stands out in my mind is Paul's second letter to the Corinthians. In that letter he talks about a treasure."

Gallagher found the particular verse at second Corinthians 4:7.

"How did you find that verse so quickly? You're not a churchgoer?"

"Knowing what the Bible says and means has nothing to do with going to a church. For hundreds of years people have been reading the Bible once it became available in the vulgar tongue without attending any church. If you look at history and read about all the blood that spilled in the name of God, you can easily see the two have been at odds with one another. Since Constantine's time soldiers wore the words 'In Hoc Signo Vinces' meaning 'In This Sign You Shall Conquer' on their breastplates. True Christians, who follow Christ's example, do not bear arms and kill one another. And you must remember, I'm a book collector and what book has always been the number one best seller?"

Jonathan just nodded. "Say no more, you've convinced me."

Gallagher opened the Bible to Paul's second letter to the Corinthians and placed his finger on chapter 4, verse 7; "But we have this treasure in earthen vessels, that the excellency of the power may be of God, and not of us."
Look under the elm...

Jonathan read it to himself then comments, "The verse is even underlined. Do you think Nathaniel's father did this?"

"He must have because look what's hand written under the verse."

Jonathan looks closer. "He wrote the words 'Look under the elm'. What is that suppose to mean? I wonder what elm tree he was referring to all those years ago?"

"Most of the elm trees in New England have all been cut down because of Dutch Elm disease," Gallagher said.

"There may have been one close by or it wouldn't make any sense," Jonathan replied. "Maybe we can find the stump."

"I think we are barking up the wrong tree," Gallagher declared.

"Is that supposed to be a joke?" Jonathan replied.

"It wasn't meant to be, but think about it. Hathorne wrote those words over one hundred and sixty years ago. Do you think he would have buried something that important under a literal tree? During all that time it could easily have been cut down or died."

"What are you getting at?"

"I don't think he was referring to a literal tree; it had to be something else, which would be consistent with his way of thinking. It had to be a more permanent hiding place that could stand the test of time."

"What do you suggest we do?"

"I think we found all there is to find out here. Let's get back to Jackson and gather all the facts we have so far and besides, I'm curious how Helen and David made out."

Jonathan got behind the wheel and began driving back to Jackson, which allowed Gallagher time to gather his thoughts on what they had accomplished.

Gallagher begins relating their findings so far, "First a rolled up letter was found inside a wall in Suriname where Nathaniel's father spent the last days of his life. The letter was written on brown paper stationary consistent of paper used in the early eighteen hundreds with the Turner-Ingersoll Mansion watermark, which today is the House of Seven Gables Museum. In the library an old King James Bible was found, which belonged to the original owner, Captain John Turner. The verse at second Corinthians 4:7 describes a 'treasure in earthen vessels'. Below the verse are the hand written words, 'look under the elm'?"

"It seems like a very complex set of facts," Jonathan said shaking his head.

Gallagher laughs. "We seem destined for complexity."

***

20

Two hours later Gallagher and Jonathan arrive back at Eagle House and find a big surprise sitting in the living room; Jessica Williams and David Browning enjoying a glass of champagne with Helen, Bill and Anna.

Anna runs to Gallagher, gives him a big hug, and says, "You are not going to believe what happened."

"Where's the great pretender?" Gallagher asked immediately.

Helen reveals a triumphant smile. "He jumped ship as soon as he was found out. We are waiting to hear from the Concord police on his whereabouts."

Gallagher looks at the couple. "I'm glad the two of you have finally connected. What are your plans now that you know what we are up against?"

David speaks up. "What *are* we up against? We really don't have a clue anymore."

"What we've been able to gather so far is this; the British Secret Service for some unknown reason is after King George's treasure but a group called Royal Guardians may be trying to stop them and anyone else who may know about it."

"We think we saw it firsthand," Helen adds. "A man with a British accent jumped onto the train at the very last second after the imposter got on board. It looked like he was after him."

"That goes along with what Professor Dean Cook told you. Before we left for Salem I did a lot of research and I found out that legally the Royal House of Windsor, another words the Queen of England, has the legal claim to King George's treasure because it's hidden on British soil in the Falkland Islands; but here is the problem. Nathaniel's father turned it into a real treasure hunt. I found a rolled up letter in a wall in Suriname where he died of yellow fever. The letter describes how he and his crew found a strongbox partially buried in one of the many inlets on East Falkland Island. The letter also describes what was inside the strongbox. He mentions a helmet, a gold ring and what I think is most revealing, a letter sealed inside a glass bottle. The other clues we have is the stationary Hathorne wrote the letter on, which came from the Turner-Ingersoll Mansion, which is now the museum called the House of Seven Gables. Finally to be brief and to the point we found in that house an old King James Bible, which had the verse at second Corinthians 4:7 underlined and particularly the words 'treasure in an earthen vessel'. Written below the verse are the words, 'look under the elm'."

David looks at Jessica and says, "What have we got ourselves into? We never thought our interest in our families past and their unrequited romance would ever lead to this."

"I don't care anymore about the wedding ring," Jessica declared. "What I see here is a union that would've never taken place except by a mutual desire to have an answer to what happened on that night in 1826. I'm content now and I want us to be able to move on with our lives, ring or no ring."

David looked at Gallagher. "I agree with Jessica but in my heart I believe if John and Elizabeth were here right now they would want us to have the wedding ring and fulfill what they never had a chance to experience. Can we at least see the ring?"

Jessica moved by David's sentiment. "What do you mean by fulfill?"

David looked tenderly into Jessica's eyes. "I realize we've just met each other for the first time but I feel as though we have known each other for years because of all the conversations we've had together. I want to spend more time with you. What I'm trying to say is; I have fallen in love with you."

Jessica, failing to hold back her emotions in front of everyone said, "I knew after the third time we talked over the phone you were a man I could love and be with the rest of my life. We shared much of our personal feelings with each other and I feel the same way you do."

David reached for her and kissed her tenderly. They embraced each other for several moments. "I have wanted to do that since I laid eyes on you at the train station," David said still holding on to her.

Gallagher looks at Anna and then says to David, "I know exactly how you felt when you saw Jessica. I had a very similar experience some years ago at my bookshop and it was the beginning of something very wonderful."

Anna reached for Gallagher and kissed him passionately. Jonathan was watching everything and said, "Where's Valerie? I'm missing out on all the fun."

They all laughed together.

"Getting back to your request about wanting to see the ring," Gallagher said after everyone stopped laughing. "If the gold ring is truly part of King George's personal treasure you may only see it because if you desire to keep it you would be putting yourselves in great danger after considering what we know about the Royal Guardians."

"Can you explain it again in more detail?" David asked revealing some confusion.

"Okay, I believe the British government may be after the treasure for economic and political reasons. I am sure there was more to the treasure than a gold ring, a helmet and a mysterious letter. The man who was impersonating you is most likely an MI6 agent working for the British government and he knew of the existence of an inscription on the ring because he had confiscated your uncles John's diary. It said, if I remember correctly it was once the 'property of a King'. I suspect the man pursuing the agent that jumped onto the train is working for the Royal House of Windsor and a member of the secret organization of special police called the Royal Guardians. This man has not seen the inscription on the ring but must have a good idea what it says on it because why else would the Royal House of Windsor be so interested in the ring? Neither one of them have the clues we found in Suriname and Salem so I am afraid our movements will be closely observed from now on because the British government wants to find the treasure but I believe the Royal Guardians are only concerned about finding the letter that was found with the ring. The publicity about finding the ring has stirred all this up. They must know this letter is tied in with the ring and most likely the helmet."

"I can understand the British government wanting to find the treasure but what's so important about the Royal Guardians finding the letter?" David asked still confused.

"If the British government knew where to look, the treasure would have already been found years ago so they need to know what we know because they have been trying to find it ever since it was lost at sea. We now know Hathorne's crew of twenty seamen are the ones who died trying to find it in 1808. It may have been by the hands of the Royal Guardians. It was kept from the public eye because of an official letter written by King George himself requesting the incident be kept out of the news."

***

After they had all dined, they retired to the living room for coffee and dissert.

David was still thinking about all they had talked about earlier and still had many questions. He directed his next question to Gallagher. "I'm not unaware of the British governments intelligence agencies they use to protect their interests. I had spent some time studying British law at Harvard. In all that time I have never heard of the Royal Guardians and as I think more on it, the British government and the Royal family would have the common goal to protect the interests of Great Britain."

"In a perfect world all the pieces can fit together harmoniously but sadly it's not a perfect world," Gallagher replied. "Whatever the reasons why the two agencies are working against each other is anyone's guess but I do have a theory."

"What is it?" Jessica asked.

"It's a little complicated but when I attended Oxford University I took a course of study that taught the history of the British monetary system. My fascination with history was the reason why I took it. Some would call it a tiresome subject. However, when I learned about all the wars, which took place since the beginning of time; money and religion have been the major catalysts for the bloodshed. From 1750 to 1870, wars within Europe as well as an ongoing trade deficit with China drained silver from the economies of Western Europe and the United States. Coins were minted smaller and smaller in numbers, and there was a proliferation of bank and stock notes used as money.

In the 1790s, the United Kingdom suffered a silver shortage. It ceased to mint larger silver coins, instead issued "token" silver coins, and over struck foreign coins. With the end of the Napoleonic Wars, the Bank of England began a massive re-coinage program that created standard gold sovereigns, circulating crowns, half-crowns and eventually copper farthings in 1821. The re-coinage of silver after a long drought produced a burst of coins. The United Kingdom struck nearly 40 million shillings between 1816 and 1820, 17 million half crowns and 1.3 million silver crowns.

In 1819, the Act for the Resumption of Cash Payments that was set in 1823, as the date for resumption of convertibility happened by 1821. Throughout the 1820s, regional banks issued small notes. This was restricted in 1826, while regional branches were set up the Bank of England. In 1833, the Bank of England notes became legal tender and redemption by other banks was discouraged. In 1844, the Bank Charter Act established that Bank of England notes as fully backed by gold and they became the legal standard. According to the strict interpretation of the gold standard, this 1844 act marked the establishment of a full gold standard for British money."

Jessica looked at David. "Can you believe him?"

"What do you mean?"

"How can anyone know all that, the dates and the order of events; it's amazing."

Helen, who had remained quiet during Gallagher's performance finally spoke up and said with a smile, "Gallagher is a product of his grandfather who instilled in him the thirst for knowledge."

"He told me knowledge can be a protection. Whatever a man takes into his mind by reading and study will become his possession to use when the need arises. You cannot recall what never was learned. Since this whole thing began I've been brushing up on my knowledge of British history."

"What does it mean in this case?" David asked.

"Getting back to my theory, if the British government gets their hands on the tremendous wealth contained in King George's treasure, which was known to be made up of several tons of gold coins and ingots. It could change the current monetary system in Europe. It could ultimately lead to more bloodshed."

"You mean war?" Jessica asked with a tone of sadness in her voice.

"I mean war. The very reason one of King George's ships was off the coast of Cape Horn back in 1795 was to hide the treasure from France where war was going on with Britain. The Spanish interrupted England's quest to hide the treasure on the British colony called the Falkland Islands by sinking the ship and confiscating the enormous treasure."

Jonathan finally speaks up showing his frustration. "For the past few minutes I've listened to the whys and wherefores for our current dilemma but what we need to know is what do we do now?"

Gallagher turns to his friend and says, "Right now an MI6 agent is heading for the Falkland Islands with at least one Royal Guardian in pursuit. Nathaniel's father died before he was able to go back and find the rest of the treasure. He sent his crew ahead of him while he was suffering from yellow fever in Suriname. Hathorne's crew of twenty seamen, who returned to the Falkland's back in 1808, did not find the treasure and as a result lost their lives because they were caught trying. It was another example of man's greed and what they are willing to sacrifice."

Jonathan shakes his head. "It brings us back to square one. Where is this 'elm' Hathorne was referring to?"

"According to the letter Hathorne wrote, he returned to Salem after finding the strongbox and its contents around the year 1800. During that time, his wife gave birth to Nathaniel in 1804. He planned to return to the Falklands via Suriname but it was not until three years later. Therefore, he was here for at least seven years. At the Peabody Essex Museum we discovered his personal calendar and listed various places he had traveled throughout the White Mountain area."

Gallagher then stops for a moment to think.

"What are you thinking? I know that look of yours."

"We have the information we need," Gallagher said confidently.

"We do?"

"We must be too tired to think straight."

"What do you mean?" Jonathan asked growing impatient.

"You even said it yourself. You thought it was an odd name for an Inn."

Jonathan hit himself on the side of the head. "I don't believe I didn't connect the two. The 'Under the Elm' clue we found written underneath the scripture we found in the Bible."

While Gallagher and Jonathan were piecing everything together, Helen's memory again was tested. She suddenly gets up and goes into

Gallagher's study and comes out with an old travel guide. "I remember my father taking my brother Robert and me on vacation one summer to Northwood Lake. We stayed at a bed and breakfast, which was near Northwood State Park."

Helen hands the guide to Gallagher. "The address is right here but I'm afraid it's been out of business for years."

Gallagher looks at the date listed on the guide. This travel guide is old. It's dated 1938. Gallagher reads it aloud: "Under the Elm - Bed and Breakfast. The address is 308 Ridge Road, Northwood, New Hampshire. Samuel Sherburn built it in 1781. What remains today from the original structure are the current dining room and the buildings mantle and axe-hewed beams remain and have aged beautifully according to this travel guide. David Bennett completed the current structure in 1820. It's a sixty-six mile drive from Jackson to the bed and breakfast."

David gets up and wanders over to the window overlooking the valley below. "If that is all that was left back in 1938 what can be there now?"

Jessica joins him. "What are you thinking?"

"What could really be there after all these years? That scripture in the Bible says 'a treasure in earthen vessels'. I am having a difficult time believing the letter to be the treasure. What could it possibly reveal?"

"Could be a map to a treasure."

Gallagher then walks over and puts his hand on David's shoulder. "Hopefully we will find an earthen vessel containing the answer. But before we go on another treasure hunt I want to talk with this Professor Cook."

"I guarantee he will know what this is all about," Helen declared.

David looks at Jessica. "Let's get on with our lives and let Gallagher and Jonathan sort out this mystery; it's really beyond you and I."

Jessica nods her head. "I agree, it doesn't matter anymore. What matters is; you and I can nurture the love we have developed for each other and fulfill what we could call our family's legacy."

Gallagher smiles after hearing her words, walks into his study, and brings out the ring he had previously retrieved from the museum. "I want you both to have this because it truly belongs to the both of you. If the ring belonged to a Queen at one time, it makes it all the more special for you to have it. Whether, David's great uncle John stole the ring or not, he sacrificed his life for the love he had for Elizabeth. Ever since I have learned about the ring and its origin, I have thought of this possibility. The reason why Nathaniel never mentioned anything about the ring to Sophia or to anyone else is that he may have wanted his friend John to keep the ring after he knew he had stolen it, which was in 1824. Nathaniel had not even met Sophia until 1837 and did not propose to her until 1839. It was not until the year 1842 when they finally married. Sophia was never the intended receiver of the ring because he did not even know her at the time. The Peabody's quest to find the ring was a misguided endeavor."

David showing some concern says, "Do you think it's safe to have the ring knowing the Royal Guardians are out there somewhere?"

"It's not the ring they're after now that I've explained the whole picture. They want the letter that was with the ring in that strongbox. The ring means nothing to them but whatever is in that letter is worth dying for."

David takes Jessica's hand while getting down on his knee. "There could not be a better time than right now to say this; will you marry me?"

Tears start flowing down her cheeks. "Yes I will be your wife not because it's a fulfillment of our family's legacy but because I have truly come to love you with all my heart."

After the two embrace, Helen interrupts and says, "I know everything is happening very fast here but will you allow Bill and I to make preparations for your wedding?"

***

21

The next day Gallagher and Jonathan traveled up and down many narrow country roads and arrived at the ruins of the Inn named 'Under the Elm' just before noon.

"What's the plan now that we have found this place?" Jonathan asked.

"Looking at the condition of the building we might be too late. We have to find out if there are any old visitor logs that may have been stored away somewhere."

"You mean as far back as a hundred and seventy years ago? Even if we did find them I doubt the logs are legible. Why would any place keep visitor logs for that length of time anyways?"

"Well we really don't have to go back that far. If Nathaniel Hathorne stayed here at this Inn, it would have been only about thirty to forty years later when Nathaniel Hawthorne, the author, would have become famous. It's very possible, for historical reasons, the visitor log Hathorne signed might have been preserved if the innkeepers connected the two."

"That has to be the biggest long shot I've ever heard of."

"We have no choice but to search for them. I never thought I would find the very hospital room Hathorne was in when he died of yellow fever in South America; that was a long shot if there ever was one."

They both walked towards the entrance of the Inn when a voice from behind them said, "Excuse me but can I help you with something?"

They both turned around and saw a hunched over elderly man holding a pitchfork in his hand.

Gallagher eyed the man and realized he was from the farm adjacent to the Inn. "We are in the middle of an investigation and we have been directed to this place to find out whether or not a certain individual ever stayed here many years ago."

"And you are?"

"My name is Gallagher Brady and this is my associate Jonathan Henry."

"You're Gallagher Brady from Jackson?"

"That's right."

"My name is Jack Collins, the nephew of the last proprietor of this humble place. I have heard about your investigations and the museum you built up there in Jackson. It is a pleasure to meet you. Who is this individual you are inquiring about?"

"Nathaniel Hathorne."

"What?"

"Yes...you heard me right. Not Nathaniel Hawthorne the famous author but his father who had the same name but was spelled without the W."

"I don't understand?"

"It makes perfect sense you wouldn't understand. Does this establishment have any old visitor logs that go back about a hundred and seventy years ago?"

Jack started laughing. "Are you kidding? Who would ever keep records that long?"

"How long has your family owned this place?"

"My family bought this place about a hundred years ago. If there are any visitor logs dating back beyond that time, I would be very surprised. The building had gone through a number of renovations since my family bought it. If there are any records kept before that time, they would be stored in the cellar under the original section of the building, which is right under what remains of the dining room."

"Can we see it?"

"I don't believe you will be able to because that section of the cellar was closed up when the first renovation took place about ninety years ago. You would have to break through the wall to find out."

"You mean it's totally sealed off?"

"Well you are welcome to look. Let me take you down there. How important is it for you to see the old visitor logs anyways?"

"I don't want to alarm you but if he did stay here he may have hidden something that certain people would be willing to sacrifice their lives for to get their hands on it."

"Oh my...! Follow me."

They followed Jack down a flight of rickety stairs to the cellar and walked several feet until they came face to face with a brick wall. Jack hesitated a moment. "Do what you have to if it's that important. The old cellar is beyond this wall. I have been waiting for years to have the building leveled so I could expand the farm."

147

"We're not totally sure he stayed here but we found a record of his travels during the period between 1800 and 1807. He listed 'Under the Elm' as being one of the places he stayed at with his wife while on vacation."

"What about this thing you think he may have hidden here?"

"We discovered a clue in an old King James Bible that we found in the House of Seven Gables Museum. Under a particular scripture referring to a 'treasure', we found the words 'look under the elm'. With that clue and the information we obtained regarding his possible stay at this Inn, makes us believe he buried something in the cellar."

"You mean a buried treasure."

"Well it's not the kind of treasure one can imagine. But its value is like I said earlier; some people are willing to die for to find it."

"You lost me there but I perfectly understand your reasons. Feel free to look around."

"Thanks Jack."

As soon as Jack was out of sight, Gallagher immediately looked for breaks in the brick wall. "Jonathan, see if you can find any weaknesses in the bricks where we may be able to break through."

Jonathan looked over the whole area. "It doesn't seem to be a bearing wall so it will not compromise the building if we break through it."

Jonathan walked around the cellar searching for a shovel and after for a few minutes he declared, "I found a shovel and a pickax; just what we need."

They worked on the wall for about thirty minutes until enough bricks were removed to crawl thru. Jonathan was hesitant at first but eventually followed Gallagher inside the dark room. Gallagher took out a small flashlight from his coat pocket and walked towards a large wooden shelf, which had a number of clay flower pots stacked on top of wooden boxes. He started moving them around and noticed years of dust and spider webs had accumulated. He looked at Jonathan. "I think we hit the jackpot. Right now, we are literally below "under the elm", which existed back when Hathorne may have visited here. I'm looking at about two dozen clay flower pots sitting on top of a number of wooded boxes marked logbooks."

"Are the boxes dated?"

"I can barely make out the dates because of the age of the boxes."

"What years should we be looking for?"

"Anywhere from 1800 - 1807; it's going to take some time."

They both started looking through each book carefully because the pages were partially decayed from age and insects. After about an hour of searching Gallagher excitedly yelled out, "I found it! He was here in the fall of 1805. The actual day was October 2nd."

"Okay, now we know he was here, what about the earthen vessels?"

"On top of the boxes are clay flower pots; another words, 'earthen vessels'."

The both of them looked inside every flowerpot they could find but there was nothing. Jonathan shook his head in frustration. "I knew this would be a wild goose chase. Was he playing a game with all those clues?"

Gallagher kept looking around and then finally saw something that caught his eye. "I think I may have found a goose."

Gallagher bent down and picked up an old clay water jug. "I found something!"

Gallagher pulled out an old glass wine bottle. "I found the bottle Hathorne mentioned in his letter."

"Is the letter inside?"

"It looks like a rolled up letter written on parchment sealed with wax. It appears Hathorne never broke the bottle to read the letter."

"If he never read it why do you think he thought it was so valuable?"

"He may have known more than he wrote in his letter. This has to be it. We need to examine this back at Eagle House. Let's put everything back the way we found it in case someone has been watching us. I don't want anyone to think we found something."

Twenty minutes later, they made their way upstairs and saw Jack talking to someone.

They both stopped at the top of the stairs and listened. "They may give me an offer to tear down the Inn," they heard Jack saying. "What is your interest here?"

"A deep voiced man said, "We want to buy your farm along with the Inn."

"My farm is not for sale. My two sons will inherit the farm when I'm gone. It has been in my family for five generations."

"Here is my card in case you have a change of heart." The man then left and drove away.

Gallagher approached Jack. "We overheard the conversation. Is it true about your sons inheriting the farm?"

"If they come back alive. They both were drafted and heading to Viet Nam."

"Thanks Jack for letting us look around."

"Did you find what you were looking for?"

Gallagher showed him the logbook and said, "Hathorne was definitely here. Why don't you keep it? It may prove to be worth something. Maybe enough to pay someone to clear away this land so you can expand the farm."

Jack thanked them as he watched them drive away.

***

PART 2

Lies, Secrets and Rumors

22

Three days had past since Gallagher and Jonathan found the bottle containing the letter.

While Gallagher was sorting through all the information he had gathered since finding the ring Helen tapped on his door.

"Gallagher,...can I speak to you for a moment?"

"Come in Aunt Helen." Gallagher sees a troubled look on her face. "What's the matter, you look rather distraught?"

"Professor Dean Cook just called me. He has landed at Logan Airport, which comes as a complete surprise to me. He asked if it would be any trouble if we could pick him up tomorrow. He's staying at the Hilton near Faneuil Hall."

Gallagher pauses for a moment. "It may not be a coincidence the Professor had called you after so many years just at the time we found the ring."

"What are you suggesting?"

"Too early to suggest anything. I believe we will find out soon enough why he has made such a auspicious arrival."

"Oh....for a minute I thought you might be thinking he's up to something."

Gallagher looks at Helen and gives her a smile. "Why would I think that?"

***

The next morning Gallagher and Helen were about ready to leave for Logan Airport to pick up Professor Cook when the phone rang.

Gallagher picked up the phone, "Gallagher Brady speaking."

Unknown caller: *"You have gone too far with this obsession of yours and if you want your friends Jessica and David to live a long and happy life together cease and desist in your pursuit. We know you found the ring because it was so well advertized in the newspapers and we thank you for restoring what was lost so many years ago. It will soon be in the rightful hands of the Queen of England."*

Gallagher: *"Who am I speaking with?"*

Unknown caller: *"It doesn't matter who I am because I am one of many who speak for the Crown of England. We are more numerous than you could possibly know and we have existed and protected the British Crown since Alfred the Great."*

Gallagher: *"Can I meet with you?"*

Unknown caller: *"That will not be necessary; our identity cannot be revealed because we are a clandestine organization. What you can do for us is return anything else you may have found belonging to the British Crown and your friends with not be harmed."*

Gallagher: *"Where am I to return whatever things you think I may have found?"*

Unknown caller: *"You are familiar with David Browning's residence so you can leave whatever else you have found there; the house is being watched around the clock. We will leave the doors unlocked and his neighbors will not trouble you."*

Gallagher: *"What if I don't have anything else?"*

Unknown caller: *"Don't play games with us Mr. Brady. When you told the world you found the ring on Mount Willey we have been watching your movements ever since. We know about Chester Peabody and his brother Daren. We know about your trip to Suriname. We also know of your trip to Salem and your latest venture to the Under the Elm Inn. You see Mr. Brady; we suspect you have also found a very important piece of history, which must remain secret. The British government has for centuries tried to undermine the Monarchy of England particularly since the year 1707 after the ratification of the Treaty of Union. We have silenced the MI6 agent who visited Mr. Browning's home. We have also silenced many others in the past who have gotten involved with the Crown's interests. We hope Jessica and David are not next and that includes you and your family."*

Gallagher: *"If I have what you think I possess, how long do I have to get it to you?"*

Unknown caller: *"We are patient people Mr. Brady and we will give you until tomorrow noontime."*

'Click'

Gallagher hung up the phone. "I need to call our retired friend from Quantico. I fear we have put ourselves and everyone else involved in danger including Professor Cook. I don't have time to go into it right now but trust me."

"How do you expect Paul Anderson to help you on such short notice? The Professor's plane is scheduled to land in five hours."

"There are agents all over the place. I'm sure five hours is plenty of time for him to arrange an interception."

"How do you know how to reach him? He's not sitting at his desk waiting for calls anymore."

"That's where his friend at Langley can help."

Gallagher picks up the phone and dials;

"How may I direct your call?"

"Connect me to CIAWH/3 please.

"Division 3...your code please."

"Mountain Eagle 001."

"Who do you wish to contact?"

"Shadow's friend...."

"Please stay on the line."

After about three minutes Gallagher is connected.

"This is Shadows friend and am I speaking to Mountain Eagle 001?"

"Affirmative...."

"What can I do for Mr. Brady? It's been a long time."

"Yes it has and I never thought I would have to talk with you again but it's an urgent matter."

"Before you go any further I'm sure you know Paul Anderson has finally retired."

"Yes I am aware of his retirement but he did say to me if I needed his assistance for anything to call you. I need assistance immediately."

"Right now Paul is in Palm Beach enjoying his retirement. I would like to avoid disturbing the man's peace. What's your time window?"

"Five hours."

"What do you need?"

"I am planning to pick up a former colleague of my aunts; a Professor Dean Cook from England at Logan Airport five hours from now. I just received an anonymous phone call warning me if I don't deliver a certain package by noon tomorrow to a residence located on Lake Sebago two innocent people will be harmed including my own family."

"Do you have any idea who you're dealing with?"

"All indications point to the Royal Guardians...."

I slight pause on the other end....

"We will have two agents dispatched to Eagle House immediately and we will take care of things at Logan. One of our agents has just finished an assignment and has landed at Logan waiting for a flight to Washington. Where are the two individuals you are concerned about right now?"

"They are currently staying here with us at Eagle House."

"That's makes it easy. I will have the agent at Logan wait for the Professor at the British Airways terminal."

"You seemed to hesitate when I mentioned the Royal Guardians. Do you know who they are?"

"Of course we do but right now I need to get the ball rolling on my end. I will be in touch."

'Click'

Gallagher finds Helen in the kitchen talking with Anna. "We have no time to waste. There will be an agent waiting at Logan to insure the Professor's safety. Where are Jessica and David?"

Anna spoke up. "Both of them were curious about where the Willey landslide took place and left early this morning. My brother Scott has some time off from the store so I asked him if could show them the area. He was more than happy to."

"Okay that's fine, they should be safe. At least we know where they are. Aunt Helen, we need to go now."

***

23

Four hours later Gallagher and Helen arrived at the British Airways terminal at Logan Airport. The planes scheduled to land in one hour. Gallagher looked around the waiting area trying to spot someone who looked like an agent. Typically, agents are not too obvious so Gallagher continued waiting patiently for the plane to land and at the same time scrutinizing every individual in his line of sight.

Fifty-five minutes later Gallagher walked over to the window and saw the plane arriving at Terminal A. People started coming through the arrival gate and Helen kept a keen eye for her longtime friend."

"What does the Professor look like?"

"He's a little on the heavy side and sports a very distinguished looking salt and pepper beard. At least that's how he looked about twenty years ago."

All of sudden there was a commotion at the arrival gate and four police officers rushed onto the plane. Helen looks at Gallagher and says, "That doesn't look good."

Twenty minutes go by. They see a man handcuffed and taken off the plane and brought to a waiting cruiser. Gallagher is about ready to find out what happened when Helen speaks up and says, "There he is!"

Gallagher turns and sees a man who fits the description of the Professor walk into the luggage area. Helen goes over and taps him on the shoulder. "Dean, who haven't aged a bit..."

He turns around and with a big smile says, "Helen! It has been too long. It's so wonderful to see you again. Where is that brilliant nephew of yours? I am eager to meet him."

"I'm right here Professor. We are so glad you arrived safely."

"Well it's a funny thing you say that because a man was just overtaken by another man on the plane who had approached my seat from behind with what looked like a knife; it all happened so fast. I had noticed him following me around Heathrow while I was waiting to board. There was something very familiar about him but I could not put my finger on it. He kept his distance during the flight until we landed, then he made his move."

With an odd look Helen said, "You don't seem fazed by it."

The Professor laughs. "I am accustomed to it by now."

The Professor then takes off his coat.

"A bulletproof vest...!" Gallagher declared showing his surprise.

"I will explain what I have been dealing with for several years now on our ride to your home."

Gallagher asks, "Could the two of you spend a little time catching up while I check out something before we leave?. "It will only take a few minutes."

Helen surmising what Gallagher wanted to find out said, "We'll be in the coffee shop."

Gallagher immediately left them and hurried to track down the police. He spotted the officers outside the terminal with a tall hooded man they were escorting off the plane. They were about ready to drive off when Gallagher felt a hand on his shoulder. He turned around and to his surprise; it was Frank Margetti, a.k.a. the Snake.

"Frank, are you responsible for all this?"

"Who else...? I had just landed and was having a drink in the bar waiting for my flight when I got the call from Langley and I was told of the situation."

"Who was that guy who was carried off the plane?"

"He wasn't able to give his name because I incapacitated him with my right fist. I left the scene before he came to. I have to leave the area right away before the authorities start asking questions. I will be in touch."

Frank turned and disappeared into the crowd.

***

24

Gallagher remained quiet during the trip back to Jackson. Helen and the Professor had plenty to talk about, which allowed him time to process everything that happened at the airport. Was the man a Royal Guardian? Was he MI6?

***

They arrived at Eagle House, Gallagher passed his keycard thru the reader, the gate opened and they proceeded up the mile long winding driveway. When he reached the top of the driveway there was a police cruiser and Scott Rawling's car parked next to Anna's car. Chief Tom Perry was outside talking with Anna and Scott.

Helen, Dean Cook and Gallagher joined in on the conversation. Gallagher spoke first, "Is something going on?" Gallagher then noticed Scott's face. "What happened to you? It looks like you were in a fight."

Anna grabbed Gallagher's arm and said, "Jessica and David have been abducted. When Scott tried to stop them, they overtook him and knocked him unconscious. When he came to, they were gone.

"Who are them...?"

They would not tell us anything," Scott said. "They were waiting for us in the parking lot at the Willey Site. We had hiked up to where you found the ring and when we got back they ambushed us as we were getting back into my car."

Professor Cook spoke up and said, "Sounds like the work of the Royal Guardians."

"They are capable of this kind of thing?" Anna asked.

"Wait until we get inside. I have a lot to tell you."

Gallagher turned to Chief Perry. "What is being done about this Tom?"

"I have all available officers out looking for them along with the State Police. They are setting up roadblocks where they think they are headed."

"Where's that?"

"The State Police figure they are heading for the Canadian border."

"That makes perfect sense," Dean Cook added. "Britain and Canada have had a long history of joint cooperation."

"Another words the Royal Guardians are on their home turf," Gallagher exclaimed.

"It means once they are over the border it becomes an international problem," Tom Perry declared.

Gallagher looked around. "Where's Jonathan?"

"He got a call from the Observer. There was an incident at Logan and he is looking into it."

"I know the incident he's referring to," Gallagher said while holding onto Anna. "A man was escorted off the plane by the police after Frank Margetti equalized him. The man attempted to kill the Professor."

Anna was startled. "Do you know who it was?"

"I'm afraid not."

***

Everyone enjoyed the meal Anna had prepared. Afterwards Professor Cook received a tour of the house because Helen had spoken often of her childhood home while living in England. Gallagher was anxious to get down to business by showing him the letter in the glass bottle.

Gallagher and the Professor were about to examine the letter when Jonathan arrived. He went straight to Gallagher's study. "I was just at my office and spoke to my editor and he is going to run a story he received from Larry Haynes who covers the Boston area for the Observer."

Gallagher nodded, "The story about the arrest of the stranger who tried to kill the Professor."

"Yes, and I know all about the CIA operative who was involved. He will remain anonymous in the article because he disappeared before he was questioned by the police."

Gallagher smiled. "It was our friend, Frank 'the Snake' Margetti."

"I assumed as much but there's something you need to see. I have a photograph of the man Frank immobilized."

Jonathan hands Gallagher the photo.

A stunned look appeared on Gallagher's face. "He is the one who masqueraded as David Browning."

"I was as shocked as you look right now."

"I'm beginning to see a connection. Before I elaborate more I want you to meet Professor Dean Cook."

Jonathan shook the Professor's hand. "It is a pleasure to finally meet you sir. Helen has spoken very highly of you to Gallagher and me. Have you had a chance to examine the letter?"

"You arrived just in time," Gallagher said. "We were just about ready to break the bottle but before we do that you need to know what has transpired while you were at your office. The Royal Guardians abducted Jessica and David. The State Police have set up roadblocks but it might be too late. They may have already crossed over into Canada."

"How do you know it was the Royal Guardians?"

"It is quite logical. David and Jessica do not have the necessary papers to cross the border but the Royal Guardians do. I think it's called, diplomatic immunity."

"What can we do about it?"

"Nothing....It is now a job for the CIA."

"Could I see the photo?" asked the Professor.

The Professor studied the photo carefully and said, "Now I remember where I have seen him before. About three semesters ago, he was a student of mine at Oxford. The specific class he had taken was Royal Lineage's Impact on History. He wore a beard then."

***

25

After examining the bottle containing the letter, Professor Cook was reluctant to break it because the letter was written on very fine linen paper instead of parchment. If the letter is as old as the evidence indicates the letter might crumble once exposed to the air. He was almost certain he knew what the letter said and who penned it because he had knowledge of the other two items Hathorne found in the strongbox, which Gallagher had provided him with on the dive back to Eagle House. The Professor brought extensive documentation of his years of research regarding the Royal family, particularly King Richard the Third.

In talking with Gallagher and Jonathan, the Professor related how he was able to obtain a letter describing what a soldier found at the battle of Bosworth Field after William Stanley treasonous act, killing King Richard in 1485. In the letter the soldier, who was an eyewitness to Richard's death, found Richard's helmet some distance from Richard's body. Richard either lost his helmet or removed it from his head while in battle. The cause of Richard's death was from at least eight blows to the head by a sword. Two soldiers carried his body away from the battlefield. When they removed his chainmail, a gold ring fell out of one of his pockets. It was the ring belonging to his late wife, Anne Neville. She had died of tuberculosis five months earlier. He always carried the ring with him in battle to remind him of her. When the soldiers examined his other pockets, they found a sealed letter. The seal was not broken by order of Henry Tudor who was Richard's successor to the Throne of England and the one responsible for his death.

While the Professor was looking over more of his notes, Gallagher went to the guest room Jessica was staying in and found the ring sitting on her nightstand.

"Professor...I think you may want to see this."

The Professor examined it thoroughly. "It definitely is the ring Anne Neville, the Queen of England wore until her death," he said without hesitation.

Jonathan was in a quandary over what they had just learned from the Professor. "Now that we know who the rightful owner of the ring, the helmet and the letter was, why are the Royal Guardians so desperate to get their hands on them?"

The Professor nodded. "You ask a very good question, Jonathan. The ring and the helmet are not what they are after as much as the letter. The ring alone is worth at least fifty million dollars in today's market. The helmet is an item that has no equal to determine its value; so another words it is priceless. Finding the ring has provided them the proof they needed to know that the letter still exists because they know the three items were together on the ship that sank off the coast of the Falklands. Their singular purpose is to prevent the wrong people from getting their hands on the letter."

"Who are the wrong people?" Jonathan asked perplexed.

"The British government, according to the Royal Guardians...."

"If the Royal Guardians think we have the letter why don't they just ask for it instead of holding two innocent people for ransom?"

"They may do that very soon but they will not expose themselves; it is not how they operate. I think they abducted your friends to use as a bargaining chip to get the letter covertly. For one major reason, I am involved. They know I will not let them hide the truth."

"What is the truth?" Jonathan asked.

"It all comes down to how history has been written. From the beginning of England's monarchy in the 880 C.E., when Alfred the Great ruled, bloodshed and corruption had also ruled. Along with the bloodshed and corruption there have been the lies, the secrets and the rumors."

Gallagher nods his head indicating he knew what the Professor was going to say next. "You are talking about the boys in the London tower."

Jonathan speaks up. "I do remember my history. It was rumored King Richard had his two nephews killed secretly so he could ascend to the throne after his brother Edward died. There was the understanding the boys may have been illegitimate and did not qualify for the throne."

"That's correct but it was also rumored Richard had poisoned his wife Anne Neville because of his desire for his niece, Elizabeth of York."

"I thought she died of consumption or what we now know as tuberculosis." Jonathan replied.

"As rumors go, the poisoning was covered up and her cause of death was diagnosed as tuberculosis."

"Those rumors were never substantiated to be truth or fiction." Gallagher added.

"That is what is understood to be the truth to this very day by scholars. What I suspect is, this sealed letter reveals Richard's confession to both of those accusations along with his admission to be the illegitimate son of his mother, Cecily Neville. That means Richard, the Duke of York, was not his real father, which would have made him unqualified to sit on the Throne of England. Not to add to all the rumors but it was rumored he wrote this confession before the Battle of Bosworth's Field knowing it may be his last battle. He was greatly outnumbered because someone who was a loyal supporter of his betrayed him."

"If he did write his confession, why did Henry Tudor seal it in a bottle instead of breaking the seal and reading what Richard wrote?" Jonathan asked. "I would think it would be to his advantage because of being the one behind his death."

The Professor looked weary after Jonathan's question.

"In all my years of research and study on the subject that is the question I have struggled with to this very day. Henry was Richard's enemy. It would be to his advantage to reveal Richard's two-year rule as illegitimate. On the other hand, by exposing the corruption of the throne of England again it would undermine the entire structure of the monarchy. This is also why I believe the British government is seeking to get their hands on the letter because exposing the truth would destroy the Royal House of Windsor today. The present Queen of England is Richard the Third's niece going back several generations."

Jonathan shakes his head. "This letter is red hot."

The Professor smiles, "If that is what the letter truly is, Richard's confession; remember it is only a rumor."

Gallagher picked up the bottle. "I think we should reconsider breaking this bottle until we find out more about all the players in this deadly game. I will bring it to the Blackthorn Museum for safekeeping. I will get a hold of my contact at Langley and fill him in on what is going on. Professor, why not get some rest? You must be tired from your trip."

"That sounds good. Maybe tomorrow you will show me your museum and bookshop."

"It would be my pleasure."

* * *

26

The following morning Gallagher receives a phone call from Chief Perry... "They released the man who was arrested on the plane with no questions asked."

"How can that be?" Gallagher asked dumbfounded.

"No one will tell us the reason. Someone paid five thousand dollars bail to release him."

"He was going to kill the Professor."

"I know. Whoever it was had a lot of clout."

"It has to be the Royal Guardians. The man who attacked David Browning was not MI6 after all. He was a Royal Guardian."

"What does that mean in all this?"

"The Professor explained to Helen and me about the organization. They are the guardians of the

169

British Monarchy. They have been protecting its very foundation since Alfred the Great, England's first king. The letter we found was part of King George's treasure and part of a much larger treasure that was lost at sea in 1795 off the coast of the Falkland Islands. The British ship, we originally thought was attacked by a Spanish ship was not part of King George's fleet at all. According to the Professor, it was a private ship commissioned by the Royal Guardians. It explains why it was never recorded in our history books."

"Why were they trying to kill the Professor?"

"He is the foremost living authority on the British Monarchy. If there is anyone who knows the importance of the letter we found, is Dean Cook. They will not stop until they have the letter."

"We should double up on the security at the museum." Perry stressed.

"I was planning on bringing it to the museum today but I now have second thoughts about bringing it there."

"Where then will you keep it?"

"The letter had been buried off and on since 1795. It's now time to bury it again."

***

Gallagher had instructions on how to get in touch with the agents watching Eagle House. He told them of his plans to bury the letter and needed back up in case the Royal Guardians followed him. Gallagher also thought it best to keep the location from the Professor for reasons he did not disclose to anyone. When asked about it he said there was no need to place the Professor in further danger.

Gallagher and Jonathan parked at the base of Cathedral Ledge as it was getting close to sunset. Gallagher had geared up to climb halfway up the ledge to bury the letter inside a large crag in the rock wall where at one time eagles had nested. It was the best place to hide it until they finished getting Jessica and David back from Canada and resolve the entire dilemma they have found themselves in since the ring was found. It would not be an easy task for an inexperienced climber to find and recover the items.

Jonathan kept watch at ground level while Gallagher ascended the ledge. One of the agents sent by Shadow's friend stationed himself across from Cathedral Ledge on White Horse Ledge; it was a good vantage point to be able to spot anyone from the air. The other agent stayed close to Eagle House out of view. Chief Perry had a half a dozen officers blocking the roads to the Ledges. Tourists were usually gone by the time the sun went down so it was the best time to climb.

Gallagher secured the bottle containing the letter inside the crag. He covered the space with twigs and shrub grass. He descended quickly and rejoined Jonathan.

CIA agents were trying to find Jessica and David in Canada while Gallagher, the Professor and Jonathan were trying to find a clue to where Hathorne buried the King Richard's helmet. The helmet took on a new dimension in Gallagher's mind when the Professor described the helmet as being priceless.

The next morning Gallagher received a startling surprise.

***

27

The earth was turning slowly towards the sun while the autumn leaves were struggling to hold onto their branches as the cold winds from the north came whistling through the noble forests of the White Mountains. The valley was bracing itself for another ski season when a festive atmosphere permeates the countryside and the time of year Gallagher always looked forward to, but the ongoing problem facing him was dampening his spirit. The Professor was a refreshing addition to Eagle House with his vast knowledge and deep understanding of the issues facing the present situation.

After a hearty breakfast, Gallagher sought seclusion, while the Professor reminisced with Helen. The clock was approaching ten when the buzzer sounded indicating a visitor was waiting at the gate. Anna looked at the monitor and said, "Hello, I don't recognize you or your vehicle. Could you tell me your business?"

"My name is Daren Peabody and I am with my friend Marie Landis. We need to see Gallagher right away. He's the only one that can help us."

172

Anna opened the gate immediately. She quickly went into Gallagher's study. "You are not going to believe this but Daren Peabody and our friend Marie from the Athenaeum Library are coming up the driveway. They need to talk with you and it appears to be urgent."

"This ought to be interesting." Gallagher said.

Anna met them at the door, invited them in, and directed them to Gallagher's study.

"Mr. Brady, we hope we are not intruding on you this morning," Daren said. "It's quite urgent we talk with you."

"Please have a seat. It's nice to see you again Marie and to finally meet you, Daren. What's so urgent that you need to talk to me?"

"Maybe I should speak first," Marie said. "I don't know what you think of me after you found out I was arrested later that day when you visited the library."

"Never mind what I think. Thinking when one does not know all the facts is like looking through a dirty window; it is hard to see the clear picture. Please tell me what's on your mind."

"The reason why I came back to the library after the police cordoned it off was because I wanted to find out if you took Chester's notebook. I could not say why I was there to the police because I have learned not to trust too many people lately."

"I guess you should not trust me because I took it," Gallagher said lowering his head.

"I was hoping you did and my reason can easily be explained. Your reputation as a patron of the arts are well known to us in Salem. Your Antiquarian Library in Jackson speaks for itself. I also have visited your bookshop, the Turning Page when visiting your valley and was quite impressed."

Gallagher raised his hand. "Before you go any further I need to know one thing; "Where does the British Embassy fit into all this? It has been a question on my mind since your arrest."

Marie smiles, "I totally appreciate your question. I am a citizen of Great Britain and five years ago my government sent me here to pose as a cultural liaison between our two countries. In a private meeting with Queen Elizabeth herself she asked me to find out what I could regarding a ring. She had intelligence possibly linking the ring to her families past. There were obviously others details she felt was best I did not know. She stressed that no one was to know of my meeting with her and the reasons for it. Not long after working with Chester I received a personal letter from someone affiliated with the Royal Guardians. They explained they had knowledge of the ring and unbeknown to the Queen if the ring was found, could undermine and possibly destroy the Crown of England. I was advised not to pursue the Queen's request. I was in a quandary as to what I should do so I became confused as to who I should listen to because I knew from my studies in school the Royal Guardians was set up to protect the Crown as far back as the time of King Alfred. In the process, I fell in love with Daren, who I actually met in England while he was there on one of his book hunting trips a year earlier. I only was supposed to be here six months but as you can see, six months has turned into five years. I felt it necessary to stay here longer for another reason. One of my duties for the Royal Guardians was to scare off Chester and Daren so they would cease pursuing the ring. By their direction I placed threatening letters in the mailbox at the same time I collected the mail so no one would suspect. As time went on I was falling deeper in love with Daren. The death of Chester was the final blow that made me realize what a horrible thing I had been doing for Queen and country. I had to make amends somehow and that's when I got caught trying to get the notebook."

Daren handed Gallagher the letter. "This was one of the letters he was meant to receive but I was able to read it first."

Gallagher read it aloud;

"Mr. Peabody

You do not know who we are and it will remain so in the future. It has come to our attention you have been seeking to recover a lost ring, which you believe belonged to your family. By your interest in finding this ring, you have put you and your brother in grave danger. We advise you to cease and desist in your efforts in this regard. We will be monitoring your activities at all times; when you are work, at home or wherever you travel. You will not see us, but we will be in striking distance at all times and we will not hesitate to eliminate you and your brother for the sake of the Crown."

Gallagher put the letter down and shook his head. "You mean you never showed him this letter?"

Daren shook his head. "I was afraid he would not handle the threat very well because of his failing health. I realized it was a mistake once I found out the threats continued as they did."

"I purposely avoided asking Chester about his obsession on finding the ring," Marie added. "I didn't want him to know I knew anymore than what he had already volunteered to tell me himself, which was to let him know if anyone inquired about the story of the 'Ambitious Guest'. I knew it had something to do with the ring. I took the opportunity while you and your wife were searching through Hawthorne's notes to ask him more about the ring. I felt I needed to know exactly what he already knew."

Daren handed Gallagher another letter. "Once I knew about the threats I started my own secret investigation. My work requires me to travel to England several times a year and while spending time there I have done much research regarding the British Monarchy. On one of my trips, I extended my stay for three months and heard several lectures on the subject at Oxford. The reason for my interest was because of this particular letter, which I found among Nathaniel Hawthorne's personal letters."

Gallagher reads the letter aloud;

Dear Nathaniel,

I write this letter in behalf of your dear father who, by his premature death, left you at the tender young age of four. He had left me with much of the responsibilities regarding the handling of his estate because of your mother's frail nature and recent poor health. You have already received much from your father's will but more needs revealing on what your father found while he was on the island of East Falkland in the year 1799. Your father was able to uncover a chest from an inlet cove on the island. Inside the chest was a gold wedding ring, which you now possess. Besides the ring, a helmet and a sealed letter was also inside. He brought back the three items with him to Salem where you were born. He hid the unopened letter somewhere unknown for reasons he never disclosed but he did leave a curious notation about the helmet. Among his personal effects, he had written under the family tree of the Royal House of the Plantagenet a small notation. The notation simply read; "The helmet-Richard?" From what I have been able to gather, your father was trying to tell you the helmet belonged to Richard the Third of England. If this fact is true about the helmet, the ring and the letter may have also been the possession of Richard, the King of England. As your legal guardian, I urge you to pursue the possibility your father found a priceless piece of history. Accompanying this letter, I have enclosed the family tree of Richard the Third.

Sincerely,

Uncle Robert

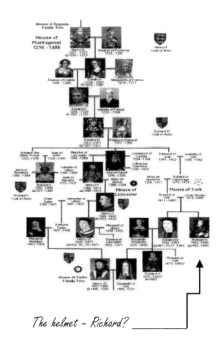

The helmet – Richard?

Gallagher looked at Daren. "This letter was from his uncle, Robert Manning. Did you find anything else of interest?"

"Yes I did. I found this homemade bookmarker inside Nathaniel's personal copy of the House of Seven Gables. He wrote an interesting message on it."

Gallagher took the bookmarker and read it aloud:

"Among the tangle wood I bury Richard."

Gallagher looked intently at Daren. "After you found out what Marie had been doing to your brother you still plan to get married?"

"While she was falling in love with me I was with her. She explained her sincere motive behind what

178

she did. She had no idea of my brothers heart condition."

Marie held Daren's hand. "The words in those letters were not mine. I convinced myself I was just the liaison I suppose to be."

***

28

Daren and Marie left Gallagher hoping he would understand their situation. They wanted to get on with their lives without having to look over their shoulders because of the ring. Daren made it very clear he did not have the same obsession as his brother did but only got involved because of his need to find out what his brother had stirred up with the ones making the threats. After hearing of his brother's death and finding it was Marie's misguided devotion to the Queen, he realized it was something he needed to abandon for the sake of his love for Marie. Gallagher could not help thinking about how the lives of four individuals, Jessica and David and Daren and Marie; were so badly affected by the greed of many heartless and wicked people. Whether it is politics, religion or just plain selfishness, some have been determined to cause much hardship and misery to their fellowman.

Gallagher joined Anna and the Professor in the living room and related what he had just learned. After much discussion, Gallagher concluded that the helmet that once belonged King Richard is buried somewhere under a tangle wood. The bookmarker that was inside Hawthorne's personal copy of his novel, The House of Seven Gables, was a clue in itself.

Gallagher called Jonathan at the Observer and told him what he had learned and asked him to find out what he could about where Hawthorne wrote the House of Seven Gables. After an hour Jonathan called back and said, Hawthorne wrote it in a small cottage in Stockbridge, Massachusetts. After hearing the location, Gallagher immediately knew what the words 'tangle wood' meant.

***

The following morning Gallagher and Jonathan made their plans to travel to Lenox, Massachusetts where the summer home of the Boston Symphony Orchestra is located called Tanglewood. Gallagher called ahead and talked with the Tanglewood office, and told him of his need to inspect the grounds for any evidence regarding an investigation he is currently involved with at home. At first, they denied Gallagher access because he was not forthcoming with the nature of the investigation. Jonathan then asked his wife Valerie who has been a guest violinist with the orchestra on several occasions to speak in his behalf. After Valerie spoke with Erich Leinsdorf, the principle conductor of the Boston Symphony, he was able to convince the Tanglewood Administration to allow Gallagher access to the grounds since it was during the off-season.

***

Helen and Gallagher asked the Professor if he would stay at Eagle House during his time in the United States. The Professor was hoping to stay until Gallagher cleared up the mystery of the unopened letter in the bottle, so he gladly accepted her invitation.

Before Gallagher left for Lenox, he received a call from Shadow's friend. The man Frank Margetti neutralized on the plane took his own life while in custody while awaiting transport to Quantico for further questioning. He swallowed a cyanide pill he had hidden in the sole of his shoe. The act was typical of the Royal Guardians who would rather die for the King or in this case the Queen, than reveal their identity. He also informed Gallagher about the agents who are watching Eagle House. He told him they would be watching the area until the Professor returned safely to London.

***

Gallagher drove south on Rte. 93 then connected onto Rte. 495 west, then the Mass Turnpike heading west. The estimated time to arrive at Tanglewood was about five hours. Gallagher borrowed a Ford Crown Victoria from the Jackson police for the trip to Lenox to avoid detection from whoever was spying out the area. He met Chief Perry behind the police station early in the morning before sunrise and took the specially equipped vehicle with its beefed-up 351 Windsor engine. The car also was equipped with a CB radio.

At five minutes of eleven in the morning, Gallagher drove onto Rte. 77 and then after about four miles pulled into Tanglewood's main parking lot. When getting out of the car they immediately saw the problem facing them; the spacious grounds of Tanglewood were thick with dozens of unique tangle wood trees; so given the name.

They walked toward the main entrance and used the telephone outside the ticket office. After about five minutes, an older man dressed in a painter's outfit and hat unlocked the gate. "My name is John. I was told you would be coming and to assist you anyway I can."

"Thank you John. My name is Gallagher Brady and this is my associate Jonathan Henry. What we would need from you is a layout of the grounds."

John pulled a map out of his pocket. "I thought you might so I drew this map for you. I was told you are interested in our trees; the unique tangle woods."

"Excellent...!" Gallagher exclaimed.

"I also marked the sections where newer trees had come up more recently."

"How recent...?" Jonathan asked.

"The Berkshire Music Center opened in 1940 and was later named Tanglewood in 1950. In the early thirties, shrubs and deciduous trees needed removal in order for more tangle wood trees to grow. Tangle wood trees are of unknown origin. They are one of the only flora, which do not have any saplings, or seeds, or any form of descendents.

Their roots simply spread, and every now and again a new tree pops up; which is quite unique."

"You seemed to know much about dendrology."

John smiles…"I only paint in the off season. I am responsible for the entire ground area here at Tanglewood, including mowing our beautiful lawn and trimming all the edges that border the property. Our trees are a specialty of mine. Just like caring for a Bonsai tree, I care for these wonders of nature."

"Well I hope we do not have to disturb one of your trees in our investigation." Gallagher said soberly.

"What are you looking for precisely?" I am to extend to you anything you need or want. I was told not to stand in your way."

Jonathan looked at Gallagher. "I guess Valerie made a good case to Leinsdorf."

Pointing to the map, Gallagher asked, "Can you show me where trees may have been as far back as 1850?"

John placed his finger on the lower back corner of the property. "These are the oldest trees."

***

29

Gallagher and Jonathan spent several hours examining dozens of trees but found no evidence of anything buried under any of them.

They returned where the old man named John was busy painting a bench. He looked up and said, "By the look on your faces you did not find what you were looking for."

Gallagher nodded. "It's like looking for a needle in a haystack."

"Maybe I could help you if you tell me what you are actually looking for."

Gallagher realized he had to trust the old man and said, "We suspect the writer, Nathaniel Hawthorne may have buried a precious artifact under a tangle wood tree. He would have done that around the year 1850 when he was living in the area writing his famous novel, The House of Seven Gables."

"Oh...why didn't you say so before? The house he stayed at while writing that book is two miles down the road. It is a little red cottage where he and Melville wrote some of their works together. Melville also worked on his own masterpiece, Moby Dick not too far from here at his home, which he named Arrowhead, in the nearby town of Pittsfield."

"Are there any tangle wood trees by the red cottage?"

"When Hawthorne stayed there he asked if a tangle wood tree could be uprooted and transported to the back yard of the cottage. I remember reading something to the effect his desire do have that done caused some interesting discussions in the neighborhood."

"Are you telling me the tree is still there?" Gallagher asked showing his excitement.

"It is there and as beautiful as ever. I maintain that tree regularly along with all these others trees. You are not thinking of digging it up?"

Gallagher shook his head showing his frustration over John's concern. "I don't know how else to find out if the artifact is under the tree."

"Is it really that important?"

Jonathan looked at Gallagher then he looked at John and said, "Two people we know of for sure will be in serious trouble if we don't find that artifact."

John nods and says, "Say no more; I understand."

***

Both of them left Tanglewood and drove west on Rte. 77 and came to a farm with the little red cottage. John said; they use the cottage when some of the orchestra's musicians want to practice in solitude. It's not occupied off-season.

They walked around the back of the house and spotted the twisted and wildly sprawling tangle wood. "I don't know where to start digging," Jonathan said.

Gallagher walked over to the car and took out two shovels and as he was walking back to the tree, he looked at the front of the cottage and noticed something embossed on the door. He walked up to it and saw what Hawthorne must have meant. The image of a tangle wood tree carved into the oak door. He yelled out to Jonathan, "I think I found the tree."

Jonathan hurried over and said, "Could that be it?"

Gallagher looked carefully at the threshold. "If knowledge serves me correctly the threshold is in the shape of a box and is hollow on the inside. We need to pry up the wooded threshold. There should be a hollow section under the casing. It could be big enough to hide a helmet."

Gallagher forced the blade of the shovel under the threshold and pried it up until the board cracked. Under the threshold, was a shallow space and Gallagher reached in and pulled out burlap sack. He carefully untied the sack and pulled out a metal helmet. On the side of the helmet was the Coat of Arms of the King of England. "We have it. This completes the three items Hathorne found in the strongbox. We need to get back to Jackson and show the Professor, without delay."

***

30

They stopped back at Tanglewood to tell John they had found what they were looking for but they found John lying on the ground where he had been painting. Gallagher felt for a pulse and said, "He's alive."

He carefully examined him and did not find any wounds or blood anywhere. He finally came to and said, "Who were those guys?"

"What guys?" Jonathan asked.

John sat up and said, "After you left a car drove up and two men got out and started asking me questions."

"What kind of questions?" Gallagher asked.

"They wanted to know what you two were doing here. I told them you were looking at our trees, nothing more."

"That's it?"

"That's all you told me so I figured that is all they needed to know. Before I knew it they clubbed me and that's all I remember."

Jonathan looked at Gallagher and said, "Royal Guardians."

Gallagher nodded. "They are probably close by. We better get out of here."

They thanked John and made sure he called the local police to report what happened then left.

During the five-hour ride home Gallagher kept looking in his rearview to see if anyone was following them. They continued without incident all the way to Worcester where Gallagher wanted to see the curator of Higgins Armory. In 1931, the Armory was open to the public and next to the Metropolitan Museum of Art in New York City had the largest arms and armor collection.

Bradley Carter Higgins met them in the lobby and he inspected the helmet. After his examination Higgins looked at Gallagher with his mouth open in awe and said, "Where did you say you found this?"

Gallagher thought for a moment. "I didn't. But if you must know it was found under a tree in Stockbridge, Massachusetts."

"Under a tree...? I cannot imagine who would bury this under a tree. This is an authentic English helmet going back to about the fourteenth or fifteenth century."

Gallagher smiled and said, "Our thinking is the same. We just wanted an expert's assessment to be sure. We would like to stay longer and tour your wonderful museum but we need to run. Thank you for your time."

They left Worcester by Rte. 12 then connected onto Rte. 110 and then Rte. 111 until they reached Rte. 93 and continued north until they reached the Kancamagus Highway. They drove east until they reached Rte. 16 in Conway. The hour was getting late so they decided to stop at the Village Tavern for a late supper. Gus Swenson saw them as they walked in and quickly walked over and said, "Chief Perry has been trying to reach you on your CB radio. They caught a man trying to climb Cathedral Ledge."

Gallagher quickly went to the phone. "Chief Perry, its Gallagher. What happened at Cathedral?"

"We got a call from a hiker and said he saw a man dangling from a rope halfway up the ledge. We quickly went to the scene but it was too late. He fell to his death."

"Any identification...?"

"That's the odd thing. He had no wallet or anything else that would identify him except a note we found in his pants pocket. It said to deliver the package to a particular address."

Gallagher, not wanting to waste anymore time talking asked firmly, "Well…, what's the address?"

"It was yours. Did I say something wrong?"

Gallagher looked at his watch. "No Tom. I'm sorry if I sound a little edgy. We just got back from Tanglewood and we found what we were looking for but now I am at the point where I do not know where to go with all this. The ring we found on Mount Willey, the mysterious letter we found "Under the Elm" and now a helmet that may have belonged to the King of England by the name of Richard the Third has me in a dilemma."

"I don't follow you."

"Because of finding the ring it has led interested parties willing to threaten and abduct any individuals who may be in there way."

"Are you talking about the Royal Guardians or MI6?"

"Take your pick. I am getting sick and tired of the self-indulgent pursuits of these people who cannot leave well enough alone. They need to get with it and just enjoy life without having to disrupt and hurt innocent people."

Tom shook his head and said, "John Peterson told me of your idealistic view of life. He said it is what drives you at times. I had seen it for myself before but not like this."

"I wear my heart on my sleeve I'm afraid. When I found out what was behind what happened to my parents and the way they died in that plane crash, I have had a passion to stop the evil that surrounds us any way I possibly can."

"What are you going to do with all the things you found?"

"From what I have been able to gather, the ring and the helmet are virtually priceless. Imagine it; the helmet Richard the Third of England wore during his last battle and the ring, which belonged to his late wife now in our possession after more than five hundred years. The whole thing is staggering and yet; it's an unopened mysterious sealed letter that's the focus of these vultures. I really do not know where to go from here."

"How about your friend the Professor from England...?"

"I am afraid to say to you what I am thinking?"

"What do you mean?"

"I'd rather not without further looking into my reasoning. I need to get to Eagle House right away."

***

31

Gallagher walked into the kitchen at Eagle House and found Helen and Anna sitting at the table having tea. Helen looked up and said. "I am glad you're back. Dean Cook is gone."

"What...?"

"Just what I said; he left right after you left for Tanglewood. He said he wanted to take a walk and get some fresh air. I have yet to call the police. I didn't want to jump to conclusions."

Gallagher looked at Helen knowing she was holding back something. "What conclusion could you jump to? He just went for a walk."

"Before he took his walk he used the phone in your study and talked at length with someone. After he got off the phone, he left for his walk. I looked at the surveillance monitor and saw him get into a car at the bottom of the driveway."

"Okay. What else are you not telling me?"

"Before he took his walk he asked where you hid the letter."

"You told him?"

"I didn't think there was a problem telling him. I mean we go back to Oxford together and we have been good friends. He's here to help us and why would I think otherwise?"

Gallagher tried to hold back but he finally had to tell Helen what he had been thinking since the Logan Airport incident. "I am afraid Dean Cook is a Royal Guardian and he was almost murdered on the plane by a Royal Guardian. They obviously were afraid he was going to compromise their identity. If Frank Margetti had not gotten there in time, you would have lost your friend. The Guardians were under the impression he was coming here to help us. That's why he was being followed at Heathrow Airport before he got on the plane."

Helen shook her head. "I cannot believe that!"

"Do not let sentiment and an old friendship get in the way of the facts."

"Explain." Helen said showing her frustration.

"After he arrived here he told us many things revealing his vast knowledge of the Royal Monarchy, which was quite impressive."

"What did you expect? He is the foremost authority on the subject."

"Yes, and because of that, I was a little surprised when he didn't want to break the bottle. If being a true student of the subject, breaking the bottle and reading the letter would be a dream come true but instead he declined because I believe his superiors did not want the letter revealed to anyone. He gave the excuse the letter was written on linen paper and should not be exposed to the air after so many years. I just talked with Tom Perry and he said someone tried to get the letter but fell to his death. He had no identification except in his pocket they found a note with this address on it instructing the man to bring the package here."

"Do you think the Professor was waiting for him at the bottom of the driveway?"

"Yes."

"Then where is he now?"

"Good question. I need to get a hold of Shadow's friend and fill him on the latest. We have the helmet, the ring and the letter. All I want to do is give it to the Royal Guardians and end this thing."

Helen thought for a moment. "What is your gut feeling about the Professor?"

"I have a strong feeling many years ago he was coerced into joining the Royal Guardians. He probably did not have a clue as to their treachery."

"But he is the one who told us about the Guardians." Helen said trying to argue the point.

"It was a perfect cover for him to bring that out to us. It worked because you were fooled and I almost was."

"Why do that...?"

"It's one of the best ways to avoid suspicion by speaking against something or someone because it rules out any complicity."

"I must be getting old or too sentimental. I know my father would have handled it differently."

"Jonas was a smart man but his suspicions are what killed him in the end."

"He was always suspicious because of his unrealistic view of life. The Thorn Hill Covenant was a perfect example." Helen added.

Gallagher nodded. "I am aware I have that tendency myself but in recent years I think I have developed a more broad minded view of life."

"Your feelings about Dean Cook are a result of your broadminded thinking?"

"Let me just say, I am not as gullible as I have been in the past. Life has taught me that much."

"What is your next move?"

"I am going to get Shadows friend up to date on our end and I am going to retrieve the letter because I found out what I needed to know."

"Wait a minute. You hid the letter at Cathedral Ledge on purpose to draw out the Professor?"

Gallagher could not hold back from revealing a slight smile. "Let me just say, I never told you not to say anything about where I hid the letter to the Professor. It was just a matter of time you would have volunteered the information if he asked you."

***

Gallagher and Anna woke up early the next day and drove to Cathedral Ledge. Gallagher climbed down from the top and retrieved the bottle. His plan had worked and his suspicions about Professor Dean Cook were correct.

Gallagher collected the ring, the helmet and the letter and placed them in the vault at the Blackthorn Antiquarian Museum. He had just updated his security system with state of the art surveillance cameras and alarms.

***

32

Two weeks passed and no word from Shadows friend on the progress of finding Jessica and David. During the same time, Daren and Marie no longer received any threats. Gallagher had mixed feelings about the calm, which now was settling over the valley. There were no more treasure hunts to go on and no more strangers lurking about the countryside. It was Saturday morning and Gallagher was elated he could finally find the time to enter the Turning Page and enjoy some time with the children of the valley.

Toby Jones, the spokesperson for the group said, "We were wondering if you would ever read to us again."

Gallagher bowed his head. "I'm sorry kids. I promise I will not let myself get side tracked again. This latest adventure was unexpected."

Just as Gallagher sat down to start reading the first page of David Copperfield, Kathy entered the reading room and said, "Gallagher, there's a gentleman asking for you. He is waiting by the front desk."

Gallagher rolled his eyes. "Have you ever seen him before?"

"No… but he speaks with an English accent."

"Oh, great…! I will be right there. Tobey, could you fill in for me? Just read as I showed you. Put feeling into the words, make them come alive."

Toby began reading chapter one; "I am born....."

The children start laughing.

Toby starts to laugh himself and says, "It sounds funny but it's how it starts."

Gallagher smiles as he leaves the room and meets the man at the front desk. He is dressed in a Harris Tweed suit, Crockett and Jones dress shoes and a Yorkshire driving cap. Gallagher felt like he was just transported to the English countryside.

"Can I help you? I am Gallagher Brady."

"Mr. Brady, it's a pleasure to meet you. I hope I'm not disturbing you."

"No, I was spending some quality time with my young friends but I have a few minutes."

He looks into the reading room and sees about ten children sitting quietly while Toby is reading to them."

"I see what Marie has said about you is correct."

"Marie?"

"Marie Landis. She told me all about what has happened recently and she thought it best I speak with you firsthand."

Gallagher eyes the man. "Speak to me about what?"

"I can understand your caution so first of all, let me introduce myself. My name is Henry Bosworth. I am here by request of Queen Elizabeth."

Gallagher's eyes open wider showing his surprise. "What have I done to receive such an honor?"

"Let me put it this way. It's not what you have done but what you could do."

"Please Mr. Bosworth; come into my office where we can speak privately."

Gallagher closes the door to his office and Bosworth continues. "As you know Marie came to this country five years ago from England posing as a cultural liaison. Her contact with Daren Peabody resulted in an unexpected romance and so she decided to stay in this country. She is planning to marry Daren. We are very happy for them both."

Gallagher interrupts and says, "Pardon my impatience but what does it have to do with me and the Queen?"

"Are you familiar with the Royal Guardians?"

"Unfortunately yes because of recent experiences."

"I don't know what those experiences may be but the Royal Guardians are not sanctioned by the Royal House of Windsor. It is a known fact the sect was formed by order of Alfred the Great to serve as protector of the Crown. In time, the sect grew much larger and became a force, of its own volition; to the point of becoming an enemy to the Crown for its own selfish gains."

"Let me speak plainly," Gallagher interrupted. "I am not going to beat around the bush because I am not naïve to think you are unaware of the three items we have discovered recently, which may indeed have belonged to Richard the Third of England."

"You are right in your thinking."

"Is the Queen interested in acquiring these items?"

"No she is not!"

"Then what is this all about?"

"She would like to use your abilities to shut down and destroy the Royal Guardians once and for all."

Gallagher shakes his head. "Why me...?"

"She heard about your involvement in shutting down the Fifth Column organization called the 'Cause', which had also been a thorn in side of the Crown and the British Government since Hitler."

"You're kidding me."

"Not in the least. You have the ability to work invisibly where MI6 and MI5 have too much of a signature on the world seen. The three treasures you have unearthed have eluded the Royal Guardians since the sinking of the British ship off the coast of the Falklands in 1795. You can use them as bait so the nucleus of the sect can be destroyed."

"You are talking about a very risky assignment. Why do you think I would even want to get involved in such a deadly game?"

"What I am about to tell you will stagger your imagination.

"Should I sit down?"

"It would be a good idea. You wouldn't happen to have some tea?"

"By all means; we have a small café next to our reading room. Just give me a moment."

Gallagher walked out of his office and walked over to Kathy who was overseeing the children in the reading room. "How are they doing?"

Kathy smiled. "Toby is really getting into it. I think you have turned him into a regular orator. He is reading with good modulation and sense stress like you taught him."

"Great. Would you mind making my guest and me some tea?"

"Earl Gray?"

"But of course."

***

Gallagher eager to hear what Mr. Bosworth had to say said, "I am now ready for you to stagger my imagination, but let me tell you, it will take some doing. I have been involved in a series of unbelievable events ever since I found the gold ring."

"It all goes back to the year 1810. King George the Third received an unusual letter from a native from the East Falkland Islands. The native, who was an educated man, was able to give the letter to the Captain of a British merchant ship while in port. The Captain promised he would deliver the letter to the King as soon as they docked in England. One thing he mentioned in the letter was this interesting fact; a man and his crew while docked at Port Stanley found a chest containing a gold ring, a helmet and a letter sealed inside a glass bottle. The man who remained anonymous never broke the bottle that contained the letter so he never read it. The seaman that the native talked with said the ring, the helmet and the letter went back with the unknown man to Massachusetts and he hid the letter and the helmet."

Gallagher's memory kicked in and said, "This native mentioned, was his name Louis?"

"Yes it was. How do you know that?"

"One of those unbelievable events I mentioned was when I found the deathbed of Nathaniel Hathorne who was the father of the famous author Nathaniel Hawthorne in Suriname. I was able to find the hiding place where he kept a very revealing letter. Before he died of Yellow Fever, he had written down his exploits while in the Falkland Islands and in the letter he mentioned a native named Louis."

"You are making this much easier than I expected," Bosworth declared with a smile. "In the letter Louis told about the chest Hathorne found and what he told Louis it contained. Louis wanted no part of any treasure and promised he would remain silent about the discovery. Louis heard about Hathorne's illness from one of his crewmembers when they landed back in East Falkland to recover more of the treasure. Not long after that, Hathorne's crew were massacred; all twenty of them by Royal Guardians."

Gallagher's mind was racing. "So what I think you are telling me is, the Royal Guardians are not working for the interests of the Royal Monarchy."

"That's correct. They are mercenaries with the sole purpose of robbing and pillaging anything attached to Crown of England. The British ship that was attacked in 1785, was actually a Royal Guardians ship flying the British flag and fleeing England after stealing King George's treasure. They used the war with France as a perfect cover for their crime. King George heard about the massacre of the twenty seamen and offered his sincerest condolences to the families. He was able to get the family names from the harbormaster at Port Stanley."

"I know about the letter," Gallagher said. "The father of one of the seaman was the chief editor of our own Jackson Observer. It had remained secret as the King requested."

"Well I guess I am talking with the right person as Daren and Marie had said without question."

Gallagher scratches his head. "So getting back to the beginning of our conversation; how am I supposed to stop the Royal Guardians? As big as the Fifth Column group was that I helped shut down, the Royal Guardians seem to be a much larger and more dangerous organization to deal with."

"Like I said earlier, our MI5 and MI6 agents are not capable of accomplishing the Royal Guardians demise but we believe you can with the resources you have used in the past."

"There's another problem," Gallagher added. "The Royal Guardians have abducted a young couple who have innocently got themselves involved in this whole sordid mess. Is there anyway your Embassy could intercede and help this couple?"

"I'm afraid that's out of the question. We do not have resources to identify who the members of the Royal Guardians are and that has been our dilemma for centuries. If I was to liken it to other groups, I think of the Cosa Nostra or more commonly referred to as the Sicilian Mafia."

"I see. I have one more question before I decide if I should get involved in your Queen's request. How do I know I can trust you?"

Bosworth expresses a slight smile. "You won't know until you get involved."

"I'm not one to gamble."

"It's your choice. I am just a messenger and unfortunately, I have no way of convincing you I am telling you the truth. What good would it serve for me to lie to you? I suspect, I have been watched ever since I arrived in your valley. It's one of the reasons why I came to your bookshop instead of your home."

"I'm sorry if I am being suspicious but I have come to learn through my experiences, many people are not what they appear to be. It seems everyone has a secret agenda."

"You are not only suspicious but extremely cynical."

"I have been accused of that flaw before. I have tried to shake it off my shoulder but something always comes up that makes it futile."

"Well Mr. Brady, I hope you choose to help us. All I can do is to assure you of our good intentions in wanting the Royals Guardians destroyed once and for all by giving you this."

Bosworth holds out a small box. "We want you to have this. It will come in handy."

Gallagher takes the box, opens it and reads the message inside. "I have never heard of this before," Gallagher exclaims.

"There have been only ten individuals since Alfred the Great to receive such an honor. I hope this will help convince you of our need for your assistance."

Gallagher holds the item in his hand and then looks at Bosworth. "I will do what I can, as soon as I can; you have my word."

"Well then my work is done here. I bid you a good day and best wishes to you and your family."

Bosworth leaves the bookshop and never seen again in the valley.

***

33

Two weeks later Gallagher receives a call from Shadow's friend.

"Gallagher..., we located the couple you informed us about and they are being held prisoner in a warehouse in a small town in Quebec called Magog. We have agents staked out throughout the town. There has been very little movement but it appears the couple is all right. We see delivery trucks bringing food in from time to time so one of our agents paid one of the drivers to let him deliver a pizza. While inside the agent noticed the couple were confined to a small room, which has a viewing window and were being watched at all times by at least four men."

"Why don't you just storm the place?" Gallagher asked.

"We can't get involved just like that because it would cause two unfortunate results. We would expose our hand in Canada and it would prevent our finding whoever the top dog for the Royal Guardians is."

"What do you suggest?"

"Has Mr. Bosworth been in touch?"

"Yes but how do you know who he is?"

"We have worked with him before. He is not what he appears to be. He was at one time a double 0 agent for MI6. The British Government revoked his license to kill because of an incident that has remained top secret. The Queen took advantage of the situation and covertly hired his services to spearhead the ultimate destruction of the Royal Guardians."

"Oh...that explains it," Gallagher said.

"Explains what...?"

"A gift I just received. Apparently Bosworth wants me to work for him in finding and destroying the Royal Guardians but I don't have a clue on how to go about it."

"As you know we can't help you but there is one who can and is willing to help, your friend and mine, Paul Anderson a.k.a. the Shadow."

"How did you manage to get him to leave Palm Springs?"

"You have undoubtedly left a remarkable impression on Paul and he's willing to help you in your quest to rescue the young couple."

"Is that all?"

"You are very perceptive Gallagher; I should know that by now. Ten years ago a Royal Guardian gunned down one of Paul's closest friends on the bureau in cold blood while waiting for his daughter to get out of school. The Guardian approached his car and shot him execution style right in front of his eight year old daughter."

"How do you know it was a Guardian?"

"They always leave a trade mark; a Kings scepter pinned to the victim's body."

"That must be how it was known that it was the Royal Guardians who were responsible for the massacre of twenty seamen."

"What twenty seamen?"

"When this is all over I hope I can explain it to you?"

"I would look forward to that and to finally meet you but until then Paul asked me to have you get in touch with John 'Little Hands' Russell."

"What for...?"

The town of Magog has a large population of Abenaki Indians. They were the first to inhabit the region and still have a large presence there."

"Are you telling me Paul wants Little Hands to go on the war path with his blood brothers?"

"Something to that effect...."

***

34

The following morning by Gallagher's request Little Hands met him at the Village Tavern. Gallagher was sitting in the far corner near the fireplace and waved Little Hands over.

"Little Hands, I'm glad to see you. How was the fishing this morning?"

"The trout were running thick today. I caught a half dozen in just over an hour. It was a good thing too because the temperature was dropping fast. Snow must be on the way"

"That should make the skiers happy."

"Yes...,and everyone else in the valley; the shopkeepers especially."

"I know. I love this time of the year. Please have a seat. What I have to ask you would be better hearing while sitting down."

"Oh no...! Not another one of your adventures?"

"This one you might find appealing. A little over three weeks ago a group of mercenaries abducted

206

a young couple and are being held prisoner in a house up in Magog, Quebec."

"I have cousins who live in Magog."

"I was hoping you were going to say something like that. I need your help in getting them out of there and at the same time find out who the leader of these mercenaries could be."

"Do these guys have a name?"

"They are called the Royal Guardians."

Little Hands hesitates for a moment.

"Did I say something wrong?" Gallagher asked noticing his reticence.

"You're not going to believe this but I remember Mario telling about an incident he had in Hong Kong having to do with a member of the Royal Guardians.

"Are you sure we are talking about same thing?"

"I think he's the best one to answer that question. He should be at Daisy's Trading Post unloading a shipment of supplies. We were going to do some work on the farm later today. If we leave now we can catch him."

Ten minutes later they arrived at Daisy's and saw Mario helping unload a delivery truck.

"Good to see you Mario," Gallagher shouted.

"Gallagher it's so good to see you. My mother says you're on some big case regarding the Willey landslide."

"That's right and I could use your help. Little Hands tells me you had a run in with the Royal Guardians."

Mario stops loading the truck and jumps down. "You could say that."

"Do you mind telling me what happened?"

"As you know before the Viet Nam war became public knowledge Britain and the United States were sending troops to Nam during the Kennedy administration. They were covert operations to observe gorilla activity of the Viet Cong. I was attached to a Special Forces unit along with British Intelligence. After four weeks I was reassigned and scheduled to return home. Before leaving a group of us got involved one night in a card game while waiting for our flight out of Hong Kong with some Brits. I caught one of them cheating so I made something of it and called him a lying cheat. The next thing I knew I found myself in a back alley totally striped of my identification papers and any money I had won."

"Anything you can remember that stands out?"

"Yes, the one I caught cheating had a King's scepter stitched on his shirt pocket. So when I finally got back to base I found out what it meant. One of the Intelligence guys I worked with knew of the symbol because he had heard of a secret group known as the Royal Guardians based somewhere in England."

"Are you talking about in our time?"

"No he said they were known to be in the King's service from the beginning of the Royal Monarchy but were disbanded sometime in the eighteen hundreds around the time of the war with France. The King's scepter was the symbol they had on their uniforms."

Gallagher places his hand on Mario's shoulder. "How would you like to help us shut their operations down?"

Mario smiles. "You're joking right?"

"Couldn't be more serious. They have abducted a couple who have a connection with the case I am working on. Their lives are in great danger."

"Why not get the CIA involved?"

"They are but they are limited on what they can do overtly. Little Hands has an in with some possible family ties."

Mario nods his head. "You can count me in."

***

Gallagher and Little Hands left Mario with instructions to meet them at the Village Tavern at sundown the next day. Gallagher thought it best to travel at night so as not to be too obvious to anyone who may be watching them.

When Gallagher got back to Eagle House he told Anna and Helen of his plans to travel to Magog with the intentions of finding David and Jessica.

"How are you going to get through customs without raising a red flag to alert the Guardians?"

"Good question. We have the benefit of having Mario Caruso join us who, as you know, was

209

trained in a Special Forces unit. He will have the necessary equipment needed for our nighttime extraction."

Helen shakes her head. "I don't like it. You are putting yourself in great danger dealing with these mercenaries. Their survival as an organization throughout history is because of their passion and dedication for protecting the Royal Monarchy of England. Now they have switched their passion in the opposite direction and now want to destroy it."

"This is where the Professor's knowledge of their organization would've come in handy. Instead we don't know what he's up to."

Helen looks at Gallagher with a frown and says, "I'm troubled about my dear friend and I still feel he's a victim, not a villain."

"I hope your right but right now it looks like his sneaky rendezvous you caught on our surveillance camera says different."

"Is Jonathan going with you?" Anna asks.

"No, I need him here to do something that will cause a distraction right before we leave for Magog."

***

35

Jonathan, with the aid of the Jackson Observer published an article for the following mornings newspaper highlighting a public auction to be held at the Blackthorn Antiquarian Museum at five o'clock in the afternoon. The items on auction are rare historical relics dating back to the time of Richard the Third.

***

Gallagher arrives at the Village Tavern just after sunset. Mario and Little Hands are waiting in the parking lot. They both get into Gallagher's Land Rover and drive off to Magog.

"Do you think Jonathan's distraction will work?" asks Little Hands.

"I assume we will know soon enough. Right now traffic is very light and I don't see any cars in my rearview mirror that appear to be following us," Gallagher replies confidently.

Mario opens the sunroof of the Rover and says, "The sky is clear and no aircraft in sight."

***

A crowd starts gathering outside the Antiquarian Museum at four thirty waiting for the doors to be open when Stephen Rawlings appears with a sign and posts it on the door. 'Sorry Auction Cancelled!'

Jonathan and Chief Perry along with Officer Taylor watch from a distance on the reaction of the crowd. As the crowd disperses two men are seen running to their car.

"Officer Taylor, follow that car," orders Chief Perry.

***

In the meantime Gallagher is making good time towards the Canadian border.

"Do you have any idea where we are going to park the Rover before the border?" Mario asks.

"Little Hands, where did you say your cousin plans to rendezvous with us," Gallagher asks.

"On Rte. 91 right before the border there's a dirt road on the right. Stanstead, Quebec is the first town over the border. My cousin will be waiting at the fence. Hopefully he was able to get their without the authorities seeing him."

"I brought the necessary equipment to cut through the fence." Mario adds.

"According to my calculations it's about a twenty-five mile trek we have to travel on Rte. 55 before we reach Magog," Gallagher declared. "According to my contact at Langley, Paul Anderson a.k.a. the Shadow will be waiting for us at an abandoned Marina on Lake Memphre'magog."

"Is he alone?" Little Hands asks.

"He always works alone when he is the Shadow otherwise his movements would be compromised."

***

Officer Taylor returns after a short time shaking his head and says to Chief Perry, "Sorry Chief, they switched cars on me before I could catch up to them. They are good!"

"Sounds like the Royal Guardians," Jonathan concludes.

"Well at least Gallagher and crew were able to get out of the area in time," Perry adds. "What was

Stephen prepared to say when asked why the auction was cancelled?"

Jonathan smiles. Delivery truck breakdown!"

***

36

"Do you think Gallagher will be able to find us?" Jessica asks David as she huddles next to him trying to stay warm.

"I heard he's a very resourceful man. I'm sure he has something brewing. We just have to sit tight and hope we get rescued soon."

At that moment the door to their room opens and a distinguished looking gentleman enters and approaches the couple. "Are you two doing okay under the circumstances?"

David looks up and says, "Why do you care? Who are you anyways and why are we here?"

"My name is Dean Cook and you're here because the organization I'm associated with wants a particular letter."

"What letter?"

"A letter that we know exists that belonged to the same person who carried a gold wedding ring into battle at Bosworth Field."

"You mean Richard the Third."

"That's right."

"We don't know where it is and we don't care." David asserts. "You can have the letter. We were only interested in the ring found on Mount Willey because we thought it was something precious having to do with our families. But we later found out the ring was stolen property."

"Unfortunate for the two of you to be caught up in all this but you are a real asset to us because we now have the bargaining power needed to get the letter."

Jessica starts to squirm. "What does this letter say? It must be pretty important to commit such a crime as kidnapping."

"Well that's the question. We suspect the letter is Richard's confession of his illegitimacy to the throne of England."

"What does that have to do with today? You are talking about five hundred years ago!" David exclaims.

"Indeed it does have something to do with today. The present Queen of England sits on the throne of illegitimacy if the letter reveals what we believe to be so."

"You are talking rumors," David asserts. "He has been accused postmortem of the death of his two nephews along with other claims that would tarnish his reputation."

"I see you know your history."

"Recently I received a crash course from Gallagher."

"Ah yes, Mr. Gallagher Brady. I wish this experience never had to take place. I'm afraid my recent activities will soar the relationship I had with his aunt but I owe this to England."

"Is that what the Royal Guardians have convinced you of?" David asks with anger in his voice.

"I'm afraid Mr. Browning our conversation must end."

Dean Cook leaves the room and shuts the door.

* * *

Gallagher and company arrive at the dirt road off of Rte. 55 about 500 yards from the border. The three of them get out of the Rover and gather the equipment needed to cut through the fence and sneak over to the other side.

As they get closer under the cloak of darkness Little Hands sees his cousins truck parked near the area his cousin said would be the best place cut through.

Quickly Mario starts cutting the chain link fence allowing enough room to squeeze through. After they cross over Mario secures the fence so no one would suspect a break.

"Peter, it's been a long time," Little Hands declares as he hugs his cousin.

"Little Hands, how long has it been?"

"A think we are talking ten years anyways. I want you to meet my good friends Gallagher Brady and Mario Caruso."

"Pleased to meet you both. Little Hands calls me Peter but my Abenaki name is Running Goat."

215

Gallagher smiles. "Does that name have any significance like Little Hands?"

"Of course! On the morning of my birth my father was chasing after one of his goats who had escaped from his pen. He arrived at my mother's side just in time for my arrival into this world still holding onto his goat."

They all laugh while getting into Peter's truck. "The town of Magog is another twenty-five miles north of here," Peter said.

"How will we know where the Marina is?" Little Hands asks.

"My brothers love to fish like you do Little Hands so I know what Marina is abandoned on Lake Memphre'magog."

***

Thirty-five minutes later they spot the Marina. Paul Anderson signals them from a window to park behind the main building.

"Paul it's great to see you," Gallagher says has he reaches for his hand. "I'm sorry to pull you out of retirement for this mess."

"Well I have a score to settle as you were told from our friend at Langley."

"I know. What are the plans?"

"This is where Little Hands does his thing. At sunrise I want Little Hands to arrive by foot to the shore of the Lake where it borders the warehouse where the couple is being held. I want him to create a commotion as he tries to catch some fish

216

the way he does with his bare hands. At the same I want Peter and his brothers to be waiting in the nearby woods. They will have a boat ready to launch when I deliver the couple."

"Where do I come in?" Gallagher asks intrigued by the plan so far.

"I want you to literally knock on their front door while Mario and I carry out our extraction plan."

Gallagher scratches his head and says, "How many do you think are in the warehouse?"

"From what I have observed there are five men inside and two constantly patrolling the perimeter of the warehouse. I'm banking on the commotion Little Hands creates to cause the two patrolling around the warehouse to come to his aid. At the same time I want you to go to the front door and start knocking loudly. They are going ask you who it is before opening like they do with their own men."

"What am I to say?"

"Say you are looking for Professor Dean Cook."

Gallagher looks at Paul surprised. "He's here?"

"Oh yes. This is his baby."

***

37

Jonathan lets himself in at Eagle House with Valerie at his side. Anna, Helen and Bill are sitting in the living room enjoying some homemade apple cider.

"Well the deed has been done," declares Jonathan. "The ring, the helmet and the ring have safely been transported to the custody of the Jackson Police."

"Has Stephen been informed of what might happen?" Anna asks.

"He's prepared and ready to surrender a reasonable facsimile of the letter."

"How were you able to duplicate it; being so old?"

"My cousin Mary Ann had an old bottle similar to the one found in the Falkland's in her gift shop," Valerie said. "She also was able to find some rare linen paper to place inside the bottle."

"Won't it raise suspicion because the seal on the bottle will look broken?" Helen asks.

"Since the individual or individuals confiscating the bottle have never laid eyes on it before, they will never suspect the fake," Jonathan replies. "By the time they are on their way to wherever their hideout is the police will be ready to follow in an unmarked car along with Frank Margetti and his companions. Hopefully it will lead to finding other members of the Guardians."

Helen smiles. "I was hoping Frank was still around. He definitely gets things done."

***

The following morning….

Little Hands makes his way to the shores of Lake Memphre'magog right outside of the warehouse. Gallagher waits patiently for the signal to approach the front door. Paul and Mario are ready to burst in and catch everyone by surprise.

Little hands starts wading in the cold water and starts yelling like madman. The two patrolling the warehouse come running to find out what all the commotion his about and immediately Gallagher starts banging on the front door. A few seconds later a voice is heard asking, "Who it and what do you want?"

"I want to speak to Dean Cook."

The door opens and Professor Cook steps aside and immediately Paul and Mario burst into the room. The four men watching the couple are taken by surprise and apprehended without incident. Immediately Mario breaks down the door and escorts the couple out of the building. They quickly run to the shore where Little Hands had equalized the two men who came running to help him. Peter and his brothers pull a large rowboat out of the woods and help David and Jessica to get on.

While all this is happening Gallagher is face to face with the Professor. "What did you expect to gain by this stunt you have pulled?" Gallagher asks showing his disgust.

"Go easy on him," Paul Anderson says as he walks toward the two of them. "He's on our side."

"Is that what you meant by it was his baby?"

Dean Cook smiles and says, "I'm sorry Gallagher if I caused you and your family and close friends all this trouble but it was the only way I could get close enough to them. It has been my mission ever since I started teaching at Oxford. I knew the Royal Guardians had taken a different path than what they were originally commissioned to do but their clandestine activities were impossible to capture. When I heard what was found on Mount Willey through the Associated Press, which we tap into in England, I knew the Royal Guardians would surface."

"Why all the secrecy with Helen and me?"

"I felt it was the best way to keep you out of the fray. I guess I underestimated your abilities and I tip my hat to you. Helen was right about you."

Gallagher showing his relief approaches the Professor and reaches for his hand. "I'm sorry I doubted you. You played your part well."

Paul Anderson goes outside and sees a helicopter setting down in a nearby field. "Help has arrived! The chopper will take the six prisoners to Langley for interrogation."

"Is this the beginning of the end for the Royal Guardians?" Gallagher asks showing his relief.

Paul nods and says, "The process has begun. Just to let you know I just got confirmation that two Royal Guardians entered your Antiquarian Museum at gunpoint and demanded Stephen to turn over the letter. He did what they asked without incident. They were soon apprehended by Chief Perry and Frank Margetti."

"What about the letter? Were they able to get it back?"

"It was a fake. Jonathan did some quick work and was able to get close enough reproduction of the bottle and letter with the help of Mary Ann's Gift Shop."

"Great, that was brilliant. What about the Professor?"

"He wants to sit down with everyone involved and explain what he has be working on for years."

***

38

One week later...

Gallagher was ready to have the Professor explain everything that had transpired since the Professor had heard about the ring being discovered. What was troubling Gallagher is how did the Professor know the ring originally belonged to Richard the Third. Did he know about Nathaniel Hathorne finding the ring in the Falklands back in 1799? As far as Gallagher knew, no one had ever found or read Nathaniel's letter, which he found buried in Suriname but him alone. The very fact there was a connection to a ring found in the White Mountains and the King of England was unbelievable.

***

The Professor entered Gallagher's living room after getting some much needed rest and sat across from his captive audience. Chief Perry, David Browning, Jessica Williams, Helen, Bill, Anna, Valerie and Jonathan were all seated in a semi-circle anxiously awaiting the Professor's words.

"I see I have gathered quite a group to hear my story. My story is an interesting one. It goes back to when I was in my first year of teaching at Oxford. I had received a letter from someone who was very close to this family."

The Professor pauses a moment and looks at Helen. "The letter came from your father Jonas Blackthorn."

Helen looked at Gallagher and both couldn't hide their surprise at the revelation.

Helen speaks up. "Why didn't you ever tell me about the letter?"

"Your father made it very clear to me he did not want you to know particular details described in the letter."

"Okay. I understand. He was a very cautious man when it came to revealing anything that would draw certain interested individuals to the Valley."

Gallagher started to squirm and said, "Professor,...please continue!"

"The letter came to me about the time of your first semester at Oxford. I had not met you yet but he told me what was happening in this valley and was happy you went away to England. The letter mentioned your grandfather Graham Blackthorn and how he helped in the recovery of the Willey families remains. He also mentioned how he knew of a man named John Browning and his fiancé Elizabeth Adams."

Jessica looked at David and said, "Do believe all this was kept from us?" She then looks at the Professor and says, "You knew all this and you didn't think to tell someone here in valley what you knew? How could you do such a thing?"

David held Jessica and tried calming her down. "Jessica, let him finish; there may be good reasons."

The Professor continued. "My own father told me something he had learned from his father when I showed an interest in the history of the Royal Monarchy of England. He related the incident off the coast of the Falklands in 1799 when a Spanish galleon sunk a ship flying the British flag. The ship was delivering the treasure of King George of England to the Falklands for safekeeping because of the war with France. Because of my keen interest in the subject I researched and I researched everything and anything having to do with the Royal family. I found out about an incident involving some British seaman who were massacred in the Falklands and how their captain was spared because he stayed behind in Suriname because of an illness. I found out that man was Nathaniel Hathorne the father of Nathaniel Hawthorne the famous author. In Graham's letter it reveals he knew that John Browning was the one who stole the ring from Nathaniel while they attended college together. He never said anything to anyone because he valued that friendship and knew Nathaniel was also aware of who the thief was but he also remained silent because of their friendship. With all this gathered information, I put it all together and realized the ring was part of King George's treasure. The very fact the Royal

Guardians were adamant about getting their hands on it convinced me the letter was also part of the treasure."

Gallagher finally interrupt and says, "I'm following and understanding everything you have just told us except the letter. How did you know about the letter?"

"A great assumption on my part. King Richard knew he was going into his final battle. Rumors had been flowing through the countryside that he murdered his nephews, he murdered his wife with poison and he was born illegitimately. For posterity sake he would carry his confession with him regarding those accusations."

Gallagher stands up. "Wait a minute Professor. It sounds like you believe all the rumors."

"I believe in what the letter might reveal because of the interest the Royal Guardians have in that letter. If it says what I think it does Queen Elizabeth of England sits on a throne of illegitimacy. The British government would revel in her demise along with the entire Royal Family. They have been fed up with all the pomp and spectacle for decades."

"Hold up a minute," Jonathan interjects. "I thought the Royal Guardians originally were formed to protect the interest of the Monarchy. Why were they after you?"

The Professor begins to perspire and stumbles backward but breaks his fall by clutching the arm of a chair.

"Are you alright Dean?" Helen asks showing her concern.

"I'm fine, just old and weary. To answer your question Jonathan. As I told Gallagher the other day the Royal Guardians were originally formed to protect the Crown but after the 2nd World War the organization changed direction and began to work against the Royal Family. Finding the letter and revealing what they believe to be its contents would ultimately destroy and finally end the Monarchy of England. I have made it my life's work to prevent that from happening."

"It sounds like you believe the rumors about King Richard to be true," Jonathan replies.

"I definitely do not believe in the rumors and I'm in the process of setting up a panel of experts with the Queen's permission to examine the three artifacts that have been recovered from King Georges Treasure.

***

39

Six months later...

Washington D.C.

By special request a delegation representing Queen Elizabeth of England arrives at Dulles International Airport and is greeted by representatives of the United States Government.

By motorcade they travel to the White House where several high ranking officials, historians and several notable members of academia are waiting to view, in particular, the unsealing and public reading of the King Richard's letter.

In the center of the East Room of the White House a large table displays King Richard's helmet, his wife's wedding ring and the bottle containing the mysterious letter.

While they wait for the ceremony to start Anna whispers to Gallagher, "Too bad David and Jessica couldn't be here for this."

Gallagher looks at her and smiles. "I think enjoying their honeymoon in Hawaii beats all this any day."

"I guess you're right," she laughs. "Maybe someday we can eventually have ours."

Gallagher just smiles and says, "I think they're starting. I see the chairman walking to the podium."

"On behalf of the President of the United States and Queen Elizabeth of England I welcome all in attendance. The first item on the table for our experts to examine is the battle helmet worn by King Richard the Third of England who was last of the Plantagenet Dynasty. It is documented in our history books that King Richard was slain at the Battle of Bosworth Field in 1485 at the age of 32. History also documents that Richard was not wearing his helmet during that particular battle. It has been speculated by some historians it was Richard's choice not to wear it on what felt would be his last battle. The wounds on Richard's body revealed he received several blows to the head causing his death.

Moving on to our next item to be examined is the priceless gold wedding band that was worn by Lady Anne Neville who married Richard and was the Queen of England during his two year reign. After her death from tuberculosis on March 16th 1485, Richard always carried the ring with him into battle. He died five months later still holding onto the ring.

Our next item, which is the primary reason for this special gathering, is a letter supposedly being Richard's confession to several allegations that have tarnished is reputation amongst many members of academia. Queen Elizabeth has requested the seal to be broken and the letter read aloud for all to hear. The current reigning Queen of England truly believes in her heart the letter will reveal something other than what has been speculated for years clearing her family's name and restoring the good reputation of the English Monarchy. The speculation that has resulted in much bloodshed.

A young man representing the Royal Family approaches the table and with hammer in hand carefully taps the bottle several times before in finally breaks in two. He gently holds the letter, which is written on fine linen paper and begins to unroll it. He holds it up to the light and begins reading. *"I Richard the Third being of sound mind......."*

The young man addresses the audience. "It appears Queen Elizabeth's distant cousin Richard apparently didn't have much to say."

***

Three months later....

"Gallagher ....time to get up. It's Saturday morning and the kids should been arriving at the book shop in another hour."

Gallagher springs out of bed and says, "Is breakfast ready?"

Anna smiles and says, "Your favorite."

Gallagher laughs, "Which one?"

Anna just shakes her head. "What are you going to read to the kids today?"

"Something light. I was thinking of reading Jonathan's draft of his new book."

"That's what he's been up too these past several weeks. What's the name of the book?"

"The Great Unsolved Mystery of 1826"

"What mystery still remains unsolved?"

"One must read it to find out!

The End

~

About the author.

David Firmes was born and raised in Worcester, Massachusetts and resides there with his wife Suzanne.

＊＊＊

Other books written by David W. Firmes.

The Thorn Hill Covenant©

The Tale of Two Rivers©

Made in the USA
Middletown, DE
29 October 2015